Ye Olde Book Shoppe

A Story for the Christmas Season

Bonus Story

The Last Roll on Old Number 95

Paul John Hausleben

Cover design by Paul John Hausleben
The front cover photograph is by Paul John Hausleben
The photographs of the author are by Ms. Alejandra Lopez

Published by God Bless the Keg Publishing LLC
Henrico, Virginia, U.S.A.

Published in cooperation with

ISBN: 978-0-9886336-6-7

Dedication

To the old neighborhood

Ye Olde Book Shoppe

A Story for the Christmas Season

The Last Roll on Old Number 95

Paul John Hausleben

Contents

Acknowledgements

A special thank you to whoever set up that little Christmas tree and electric train set in the window of that old store on Belmont Avenue in Paterson, New Jersey about forty-five years ago.

"May the joy and hope of Christmas Day ring out forever more! We pray that everyone continues to hear the peal of the church bells of the old neighborhood, if not in their ears, then in their hearts, no matter where they are on the face of God's great creation."

Paul John Hausleben

November 2013

Preface

This novelette was the result of two pieces of inspiration. The first inspiration was a very faint memory of a storefront located on Belmont Avenue in Paterson, New Jersey. The store was just over the Borough of Haledon border, just beyond Burhans Avenue on the left side as you headed towards West Broadway. As a very young boy, I remember the store often-changing hands and the type of goods sold there constantly changing too.

It was a television and radio repair shop, then a store that rented various items, then a store that sold hubcaps and other miscellaneous items, a myriad of failed retailing ideas that could not, or in fact, did not survive in the old neighborhood. It never was, as far as I can remember, what my old man would label the classic, typical, Paterson, New Jersey, "front for a bookie joint."

However, you never know!

What I do remember, is that in one of its many incarnations, the store owner at Christmas time, had set up a dusty, old Christmas tree in the front store window with a small, electric train that chugged around the base of the tree on a circle of tracks. I can recall, to this very day, staring at that holiday display and viewing it through smutty windows while watching the soft glow of the lights as they blinked Christmas loud and clear to me.

It brought great joy to a young boy, and I would happily dash down there after school when it was dark, to stare at the tree and the train. I remember how sad I was when after Christmas the store owner removed the display!

I often wonder why, and how, such simple things stick in our minds for so long.

This year, about one week before the holidays turned up into a full swing, the other piece of the inspiration puzzle came into place.

I encountered a few days earlier, a particularly obnoxious entrepreneur who decided to inflict pain and suffering on not only me, but on some of my close associates too.

In a sweeping outlet of pent-up frustration, I decided to create a story with the classic storyline of Christmas, a poor downtrodden soul, lost romance, and the classic, money-grubbing, character stomping on Mr. Downtrodden.

I had been searching for quite some time to find suitable material to fill in timeline gaps of the characters from the adventures of Harry and Paul. In addition, I also had a specific character in mind that I had sought to create for quite a long time. I quickly recognized that this would be the perfect vehicle for that twofold mission.

Therefore, I put a bit of a twist to it, in order to link some older stories together, then I combined it with the memory of that Christmas display in the old storefront of so long ago, and it was finished!

Take that, obnoxious entrepreneur! I guess you can tell that I had a lot of fun writing this one!

Christmas is now a setting that I have featured often in my work, and I have to admit that the subject matter often surprises me sometimes. I know that it comes as the result of wonderful memories.

Christmas in the old neighborhood was very special. I trust and pray that Christmas, and every day, in your own neighborhood remain very special too.

It is my sincere hope that you enjoy reading this little Christmas season novelette as much as I enjoyed writing it.

Thank you for reading it.

Paul John Hausleben

November 2013

Prologue

Gramps shuffled across the floor of his little apartment on the second floor of the house at 182 Belmont Avenue in Haledon, New Jersey.

"Now, Joanie told me that Paulie boy left a copy of his manuscripts here on the table for me," Gramps spoke aloud to no one.

His eyes spotted the papers on the kitchen table; he picked them up and smiled.

"Yes, here they are, oh, good. . .."

Gramps held them in his hand and slowly shuffled from the kitchen to his easy chair in the living room. He sat down in his chair, turned on his reading lamp, and put his reading glasses on over his eyes. Settling into his chair, he opened the manuscripts and glanced through the pages. Gramps laughed aloud a bit and smiled while reading; he stopped reading, put the papers down on his lap, and stared out into the air while he was pondering a deep thought.

'I will bring these papers to Chadwick and he will give me his opinion, and provide a bit of advice to me to tell, Paulie boy. After all, I do need to pick up a Holmes book or two, wish him a happy Christmas, and let him read this. He is still such a congenial and wonderful man, despite his meager circumstance. I will go tomorrow as long as the weather is good.'

Gramps picked up the manuscript again, flipped the pages, and scanned them while speaking aloud, "Now, where is it? I just love that part when they all sing, that drunken rendition of, 'Silver Bells.'"

Ye Olde Book Shoppe

Chapter One

A Meeting of Fate

Of all the times of the year, Christmas can bring great joy to many people. It can also, at the same time, bring great sadness too. For the poor, the lonely, the sad, and the downtrodden of this world, Christmas can be a holiday of dread. It is a season to revisit lost hope, lost love, and memories of wonderful Christmas celebrations that are lost forever more in a maze of old memories.

The fortunate people of this world sometimes, often seem to forget how fortunate they are to have received the blessings of wealth, family, friends, and love. Some of these misguided folks never stop, even at a special time such as Christmas time, to count their blessings, and realize just how lucky and fortunate they really are. They look down upon the less fortunate and in many cases, try to take advantage of them, to promote their own wealth, or needs.

Yet, underneath it all, some less fortunate people prevail, they charge on and keep the faith, while staying the course no matter what the circumstance of their lives happens to be. The poor, the subjugated, those people who are down on their luck, and in need of a break, but still, they keep their faith secure and strong. You will not find the true measurement of a person's wealth in a bank account. You will find it in their spirit.

The poor shepherds in the fields, watching their flocks by night, the outcasts of society, the ones who other people did not want to be around, were in fact, the first to hear of Christmas joy, the chosen audience of the good news before all others. Not the rich gentry, not the wealthy, but the lowly shepherds. . ..

You cannot help but think that for these poor folks, this is really why we needed Christmas in the first place.

"Twelve December 1973. My Dearest Chadwick," Chadwick B. Ripplewood Jr. began to read the letter aloud to himself, while standing in the center of his bookstore located at 782 Belmont Avenue in Paterson, New Jersey in early December 1976.

He continued, "I regret that we had to part with each other's company under such difficult circumstances, but please be assured, I vow someday to return to your arms. Until then, I know you will hold me in high esteem, and even though we will be apart, our love will transcend both time and distance, and it will survive. Until I can return, I will write to you as often as my time allows, and perhaps even a long-distance telephone call or two, but you will never be far from my mind and my heart. As soon as I am able to stabilize the family estate and a precarious situation here in Sherwood, I will return to you. I look forward to that day and moment, and together we will read from those leather-bound classics, and share white wine and cheese. Perhaps, we can read a classic Christmas tale together on a quiet Christmas Eve. Until then, with all of my love, Grace Pickering"

Chadwick B. Ripplewood Jr. sighed, carefully folded the letter, and placed it back into the envelope. He then walked back to his small office in the rear of the store, opened the middle desk drawer, and carefully placed the envelope back into the spot where it had laid for three long years, tucked into a deep far corner of the drawer, and in his life. Chadwick looked down, and then he pulled out the chair from his desk and slumped into it. He just could not believe how long the hopes of that joyful reunion had lingered.

Regardless, he continued to pull out the old letter and read it on occasion, as if to reassure his heart that the entire episode of his life was indeed true, and it did happen.

It now was about three long years, and still, his beloved Grace had never returned from her native England. Three horrible, long years, and so much of life now passed by them both. His spirit was broken and his heart, well, perhaps, the word *broken* summed it up, but in reality, he still held out hope. For some reason, he clung to a thought, a dream, a wish that someday she would walk through the front door of his little bookstore, and her beauty would shine all around her, while joy would fill his heart.

Maybe someday, but it looked as if today was not going to be that day.

Chadwick looked up at the clock, and he sighed as he slowly rose from the chair, took his keys out of his pocket, walked through his store, and locked the front door. Another day done, and he knew today's till was quite shallow. He remembered only two shoppers in his store the entire day, one sale, and one shopper who just browsed, and then left. It was a typical day and all of them seemed as if lately they ran together.

It was the first few weeks of the Christmas season, and Chadwick still enjoyed the holiday; it was his favorite time of year. When all your days felt as if they were the same, the twinkle of Christmas lights, and the promise of a savior for all humankind, broke up the daily grind, and still inspired Chadwick B. Ripplewood Jr.

He reached down and plugged in the little Christmas tree displayed in a small alcove in the front window of his store. He then turned on a little electric train that chugged around on a circle of tracks at the base of the tree, plugged in some twinkling strings of colorful Christmas lights lining the windows, and shut off the overhead lights in his store.

It was early December, and in the heyday of Ye Olde Book Shoppe, he would keep the store open for a rush of yuletide shoppers. But those days were now long since gone and forgotten.

He was closing up for the day, and he would go home now. It was not as if he had to go far since his little apartment happened to be right on top of the Ye Olde Book Shoppe. He had a very short commute!

Up the staircase he slowly walked, up the stairs to his apartment. He would open a can of soup, and then retire early. It was just about the same thing, which he did every single day.

Chadwick B. Ripplewood Jr. was about forty years of age or thereabouts. He was tall and thin. He had just a patch of thin blonde hair left of his once full mane, but he still was very handsome. He had bright blue eyes, which sparkled whenever Chadwick spoke of things he loved.

In the old neighborhood, his reputation was solid and people would describe him as an honest man, and that he was a kind and caring individual. He kept a very small circle of friends; one or two folks that he knew from his church, but upon close examination, it would be a bit of a stretch to consider them friends. One would say that "acquaintances" might be a much better description. In actuality, Chadwick B. Ripplewood Jr. had no friends, he had no living relatives, but he still had spirit, he had hope, and he clung to dreams and memories.

At Christmas time, dreams and memories come back to us much stronger than they tend to do at any other time of the year.

His father had operated Ye Olde Book Shoppe for close to thirty years. Mr. Chadwick B. Ripplewood Sr. took over the store from his own father, who had started the store on this very location in northern Paterson, such a long time ago. It was a small storefront, located on one of the main routes through the city, and it was a fixture for so long in this neighborhood that people often overlooked the little store, and took it for granted. Chadwick inherited more than just the bookstore from his family; he also inherited an intense love of reading and books.

It was his passion, and it was a part of him, something he grew up with, and he would not change or trade it for anything. He loved books, the smell of them, the lure of the adventures, characters, and tales hidden within the pages.

His education ended with high school, however, what he learned from reading, a person could never measure or fathom. Surely, his intelligence level was quite high, but from reading, he acquired knowledge in almost every aspect of life. Books on dusty, old racks had been his professors, and Chadwick felt that it was a shame that in today's modern world, people have lost sight of the joy and opportunity that a book can bring to your life.

Chadwick's grandfather had emigrated from England just before the big wars, and settled in this small section of Paterson, where there was a small enclave of English, Welsh, Irish, and Scottish families. There were very few remnants left of the heritage of the old guard of the neighborhood. For instance, the "Widow's Pub" on the corner, a few blocks away from his store, was still a popular hangout for the neighborhood folks, but most of the people in the neighborhood, did not even remember that the public house had a real name! They began to call it the "Widow's Pub" when the owner passed away, and his wife stepped in and operated the business after her husband died, but the real name was now lost to most folks, but not to Chadwick B. Ripplewood Jr.! He still called it by the actual name of "The Foxes' Den."

So many things had changed over the years, and now except for the Henson family, just over the border in Haledon, and Mr. Alcott, who lived with the Hensons, most of the English folks had either passed away, or moved far away.

Chadwick was a quiet man, he lived a simple life, and he knew that many things changed over the years, but he felt he would try to operate his store until the day he would leave this good old earth, unless something or someone came along to change his mind. The store sold used books, and at one time, before the big malls opened up on the highway, the little store did a booming business. His family made a good living here for many years, invested wisely, lived frugally, and Chadwick had inherited just enough money to make it day-to-day for the rest of his life.

The store income meant very little to him now. He lived frugally off investments, and he was very careful to not overspend. He scraped by each day and counted his pennies. Luckily, he owned the building, where the store occupied the lower floor. There was a small apartment above the store, and a large, vacant lot next to the store on the end of the city block. The Ripplewood family bought the land a long time ago in hopes of adding onto their building to expand the store, and the living space above it, but the plans never reached fruition.

Times changed, and demand for used classic books and paperbacks, sadly faded.

Chadwick reluctantly brought used school textbooks in his store inventory as a primary means of keeping some sort of sales in the store. There were two or three local colleges, and a nursing school within a few miles of the bookstore, and by wheeling and dealing used textbooks, Chadwick had managed to carve out a small niche of business to keep his store operating.

Used textbooks were not his love, but they generated foot traffic, produced some solid margins of profit and they were something to keep his store operating. Chadwick enjoyed the classics. And they were his true love. They always would be. He still read and loved all the classics by Dickens, Kipling, Frost, Conan Doyle, and London. All of them! It was those types of books and authors that he coveted the most. Sometimes, he wondered if the classics and all that they meant would be lost forever.

He cherished the times when Mr. John Alcott, the neighbor from up the road, would wander down to his store; they would sip tea and chat about his home in England. John would tell of a myriad of adventures and wonderful stories, and they read together. He was a special man, with close ties to his own heritage. Mr. Alcott would on occasion bring his grandson along or his granddaughter, and they would read along too.

His grandson, Paul John Henson, was a sharp young man, and he enjoyed his visits, but the young man had grown up right under his eyes and no longer stopped by as often, if ever. Mr. Alcott had now grown old and slightly feeble, and he seldom saw the old chap anymore. Occasionally, Chadwick would spot young Paul John Henson, pass by the store and he would wave, and Chadwick would smile and wave back. He always felt the young man would go on to do great things.

Chadwick wondered why folks did not tell stories to one another anymore, and he hoped and prayed that someone, someday, would carry on the tales of this wonderful old neighborhood. Underneath the grit, he knew there was much to tell.

How Chadwick missed those golden times.

Now, he sat alone in his small apartment, he listened to music and he read. He did not need much, he was not one for television viewing, he found that most of the shows insulted his intelligence, and he was not a sports fan. He lived a simple life with the bare necessities. In fact, he did not even own a car. He could not afford to buy or keep one. He took the city bus everywhere, or he walked.

It was a meager life now. It was quiet, lonely, and subdued, but it was all Chadwick had now, since his beloved Grace Pickering left. Three years ago, this week, she left, with the now fading promise to return. A promise that Chadwick clung to, and that he was grasping at now, but nonetheless, he still clung to it.

In his mind, the lovely Grace Pickering was worth it!

Chadwick opened a can of soup, dumped the contents into a pan, and slowly stirred it while he heated it over the flame of his small cooker. As he stirred, his mind wandered back to when she first came into his life.

It was a perfect late summer afternoon when she walked into his store. He remembered the feeling that he received when he first set his eyes upon her. Sitting behind his sales counter, he looked up when the front door opened, and as she walked, both into his store and into his life. Grace was a brown-haired beauty, a woman of very rare and striking appearance. She may have been a year or two, or perhaps maybe even three years younger than Chadwick B. Ripplewood Jr. was, but not too much more.

Oh my, oh my, she was a captivating woman! Chadwick had never seen a lovelier woman.

Grace Pickering had a classic long neck, a perfect female figure, and dark brown eyes with a smile, which could melt the hardest of hearts. Perfect features, a soft voice, flavored with an English accent, and mannerisms that told you, she was a woman of refinement, but perhaps, she had a bit of adventure in her soul too.

She had come into his store on this wonderful afternoon, inquiring as to the availability of a particular book. She wanted to find it in an authentic, hardcover edition. She was searching for a classic, and she quickly found out that she was in luck! Chadwick B. Ripplewood Jr. had a copy of exactly what she was looking for on this summer afternoon, and her search was now over, in more ways than one.

Chadwick struck up a conversation with the lovely woman, and he learned that they had much in common. Surprisingly, what started as a discussion about their mutual love of the classic novels graduated to subtle inquiries as to the origins of her enchanting English accent, and her reason for visiting the old neighborhood.

Upon her telling Chadwick that she was visiting relatives here, and intended to investigate a more permanent move, "across the pond," Chadwick surmised that she might know some English or Welsh folks that had lived here for many years. Sensing an angle to keep the conversation going with the captivating woman, he decided to probe a bit more.

"Do you know the Henson family or Mr. Alcott?" Chadwick had asked. When Grace had answered that she did indeed know them both, it was then that Chadwick knew he could share quite a bit more with Ms. Grace Pickering.

The rest of their afternoon quickly passed, as they shared tea, scones, and some freshly baked Taylor English meat pies from the local store operated by the famous Taylor Brothers. Between sips of tea and bites of pie, they shared stories of the English and Welsh roots of the neighborhood and, most of all, their love of reading.

There, surrounded by rows upon rows of old oak bookcases filled with books from every nook of the world, covered and serviced with the classic rolling ladders on wheels and tracks, the discussion grew and their love blossomed. Upon closing the bookstore for the day, Chadwick and Grace walked down Belmont Avenue to the Widow's Pub and shared a few pints together, and more laughs and joy, until closing time.

They left one another with a kiss and a promise to meet again. There on a summer afternoon, on Belmont Avenue in Paterson, New Jersey, a chance encounter for a special book, turned into a meeting that occurs once in a lifetime.

Love at first sight, well maybe, it was more as if it was destiny or fate.

The romance continued, and soon Grace and Chadwick

were inseparable. She spent all her free time with Chadwick, even occasionally working in the store while sorting, grading, and stocking books.

She was from Sherwood, within the County of Nottinghamshire, in the Midlands of England. Her family, like Mr. Alcott, had come to America to work in the silk, lace, and cloth manufacturing business in the various mills in and about Paterson, New Jersey. She had mentioned vague ties to the wealthy owner of most of the mills, ties to a certain man named Mr. Dalby. She did not expand upon the ties or elaborate on them. Chadwick surmised she had some type of employment opportunity with the mills owned by Mr. Dalby, but he did not pry. She also vaguely told him that she was staying with friends in a small house a few blocks away from the store on Henry Street in the Borough of Haledon.

As the relationship grew, they shared books, romantic, long walks in the city parks, followed by passionate nights in Chadwick's apartment. The couple could often be seen sitting in front of the store at a small table set up on the sidewalk, sipping white wine and sampling cheese. Oh my, the wonderful discussions and times they shared!

It was almost a storybook situation for the longtime loner Chadwick B. Ripplewood Jr., a beautiful woman, her interest in reading and book collections, her interest in him, and Chadwick could hardly believe his good fortune.

Now, it was not that Chadwick in his past was not without young women, who, at times, had a romantic interest in him. He was an attractive looking man. It was just that his intense interest in books, his meager and simple lifestyle with low income, and the unceremonious career choice of operating a small, used bookstore in Paterson, New Jersey, did not provide a huge amount of appeal to a young woman looking for a man to settle down with, in their own lives.

One night towards the end of November, a few months

after their relationship started, Chadwick was making bold decisions. He went to the fireproof safe in the rear of the store, spun the correct combination on the lock dial, and opened the safe. There safely tucked inside, he once more confirmed the presence of the authentic, early printing versions, and original edition, leather-bound books, which were ten of the classics from Kipling, Conan Doyle, and Dickens' *A Christmas Carol* and others.

There inside of the safe were the extremely rare books, preserved in special glass cases, encased in the safe and worth a large amount of money to the correct buyer. A few weeks earlier, Chadwick had shown Grace the astounding collection, and she could not believe the quality and significance of the collection, not only in value but also in the life of Chadwick B. Ripplewood Junior. He quietly explained the heritage of the books, how much they meant to him and his family, and despite the value, that he would only sell a book or two when he required money for a very significant event or expenditure in his life.

It was a roundabout hint, and Grace's face changed, at first, to a full flush in horror and then to a shocked look, which caused Chadwick to make a careful note of her response.

Chadwick tried very hard to gauge her reaction to justify the future that he planned, but he was hard pressed to come away with an actual verdict as to Grace's feelings.

Chadwick had only enough money to survive day-to-day; he had no extra money for large expenses. The store barely made enough money to cover the heat and electric bill and every once in a while, to draw a few dollars off for a salary here and there.

Yet, the money he required was not the entire motivating factor here. The books were also symbolic to him of his own life. Selling one or two of these would provide for stepping out of the past and a step into the future for Chadwick. It was symbolic of a part of Chadwick deciding to move on in his life. In addition, it would, of course, provide the money he required for springing for a large expense for a very special event in his life!

His grandfather had obtained the books in England many years ago, and he had vowed to his grandfather to sell one of them only for a special occasion; a rare moment in his life that would warrant parting with such a special and what was, to him, a virtually priceless rarity.

He had in mind a special occasion now, and he was going to sell a book and buy an engagement ring for a certain lovely woman from Sherwood, England.

Chapter Two

A Moment Frozen in Time

As so often happens in life, plans sometimes do not work out, despite your own best efforts.

Chadwick made the final decision to part with one of his prized books from his exclusive collection, and the next day, he placed an advertisement in one of the large newspapers in New York City. Chadwick had selected one of the Kipling classics to sell. It was the one book of the entire collection, in which he felt he could part with, and not feel terrible about selling. The classic book *A Christmas Carol* by Charles Dickens would be the most difficult of all the collection to sell.

He could not even imagine having to part with that book!

Now, mind you, this was now a desperate situation for Chadwick. He *really* needed the money from the sale of the book to purchase the engagement ring, and he planned for once in his life not to skimp, and purchase as large and fabulous a ring as he could afford to give to Grace.

Chadwick was at ease with his decision; once more, he told himself that this was part of a progression in his life. Somehow, he felt the books were part of his moving on from the past and into a new life.

He planned to sell the collection one or two books at a time and then bank the money as an investment. He was confident that he could progressively sell them to support a wife and a new life. However, selling the entire collection at once, including the Dickens' book. No, Chadwick was not quite ready for that radical of a step!

It did not take more than two weeks or thereabouts for

his phone to ring with a call from a gentleman from New York City, who represented a collector in rare books living in Europe. Chadwick assured the gentleman that this book would grade out in near mint condition, and very soon, he had made an appointment with Chadwick to send a representative who would come to Paterson to view the book.

It was now early December, and Chadwick laid the plans for a Christmas Day proposal to his beloved Grace. He just needed to settle the matter of the book, obtain the money, pick out a ring, and propose. Whew!

It was such extraordinary excitement for a man who was used to a bleak, humdrum lifestyle!

The morning before the representative was to arrive to view the rare Kipling book, a tearful Grace showed up at the front stoop of the Ye Olde Book Shoppe. Chadwick had been happily decorating the bookstore for Christmas when Grace came in. She gently took Chadwick by his hand, sat him down, and tearfully explained how a family crisis back home in England required her immediate return, in order to settle an estate, health, and legal matter involving her grandparents' land, welfare, and business in Sherwood.

She was required to return home immediately. And Chadwick's life exploded and his heart broke into pieces. Grace promised to return once she could settle the matters. After a long night of tears, goodbyes, and passion, she left.

When he was able to break away, Chadwick had called the representative of the rare book collector, and he openly apologized. He told him that he could not consider selling the book at this time, due to an "unexpected, emergency change of plans."

The representative said he understood, but he explained that his overseas collector would be, as he put it, "keenly disappointed," and if, and when, Chadwick B. Ripplewood Jr. changed his mind, he was to call him immediately. He agreed, and the two men parted on friendly, but clearly disappointing, terms.

Chadwick never told Grace about his plans; instead, he remained upbeat, positive, and hopeful of her early return. Their parting was in and amongst a rainfall of tears, lost hope, and sorrow.

It was heart-wrenching agony for the two lovers. It became a moment, frozen in time.

It was a terrible Christmas Day that year. Chadwick was lost in what could have been, and it tore his spirit and soul apart. It was the first year that he could remember, since he was a young boy that he did not spend time on Christmas Eve, sitting by candlelight at the table in his store, and under the twinkle of his little Christmas tree, read cover-to-cover, *A Christmas Carol.*

He just could not focus enough to bring himself to read it, and a yearly tradition was shattered.

As so often happens, at first, the letters and telephone calls came every week. It truly seemed as if they came each day. Then, despite the poignant words in her first letter, time, space, and distance did catch up with Grace and Chadwick. They gradually and slowly drifted apart, and the connections grew dim.

The last letter he had received from her was well over six months ago, his last letter mailed to her received no reply, and the last telephone call reported a line that was no longer in service. Library research proved futile and hope of a joyful reunion dimmed.

Chadwick poured the contents of his soup into a bowl; he took some crackers from his cupboard and sat down at a lonely wooden table with only one chair next to it. There was no need for another chair; one chair would suffice, because Chadwick never had any visitors. There in silence, he ate his dinner, dreamed of lost times and love, and sadly endured another day.

The next day, he opened up his store as he usually did. He tended to a few college students seeking some textbooks that he did have in stock, and the store actually made a surprising amount of book sales.

It was a clear, cold, and crisp December day, and despite the seemingly humdrum pattern of his day-to-day life, even Chadwick B. Ripplewood Jr. could almost sense the magic of Christmas creeping into the air. It started slowly for him this year, but somehow, or for some reason, over the last few days, it grew in intensity. He was not exactly sure why, but it did. He even pulled out a few more of the Christmas decorations for the store than he did in past years, and decorated the old surroundings in gaily twinkling lights, and festive wreaths and garlands.

He sensed an unusual connection with Christmas this year, but he did not know exactly why.

He was about to receive even more of a surprise when the front door to Ye Olde Book Shoppe opened, and in walked Mr. John H. Alcott! The old gent waved while he wobbled, but he made it to the front counter and extended his greetings to Chadwick.

"I say, Chadwick old bean, How'r'yaw?" Mr. Alcott greeted him as his gentle English accent combined the greeting of "how are you," into a twisted version.

Chadwick smiled, laid down his paperwork, and rushed to greet the old gent.

"Why my, dear John! It is so nice to see you. What a wonderful surprise!

Chadwick fetched him a chair, and Mr. Alcott removed his English derby hat and overcoat, hung it on a hook by the door, then he sat down on the chair in front of a row of books. The two men shook hands and continued the greeting.

"Would you like some tea, John? I can put a pot on rather quickly. It would just take me a minute or two."

"Oh no, bloody well, no, thank you. I dare say that if I have any more tea, I will be up all night tapping my bladder. I cannot hold it as I used to. I dare to say,

Chadwick, that—I am a bit long in the tooth these days, old boy. My daughter, Joanie, keeps me full of tea, and I sneak a beer or two, or three at night now. She tries hard to pawn those bloody, awful Dingleberry beers off on me. Since I came across the pond, I am a Big Boulder man. Those bloomin' Dingleberries are way too sweet. Now, do not tell her, eh?"

"I promise to stay quiet, John, and I will not tell, Joanie. I do agree about the Dingleberries by the way. So, how do you feel? It has been a long time since I have seen you." Chadwick now pulled a chair up close to Mr. Alcott to share in the discussion.

He studied the old man's face and he could see that his blue eyes still sparkled and although older now, he still was sharp and keen.

Mr. Alcott had an obvious disability, in that his right arm was considerably shorter than his left, and Mr. Alcott did his best to conceal that fact. However, his chest was broad and strong, and his left arm, even at an advanced age, remained large and powerful.

He was an impressive man.

Chadwick never asked about his arm. He surmised that he had suffered from some type of accident, perhaps during the big war in England. However, since Mr. Alcott never volunteered the information on what had occurred to him, Chadwick decided not to be nosey and pry.

"I feel as bloomin' well, as an old chap such as I am, can feel these days. I am in good shape for the shape that I am in!" They both laughed at the remark, and Chadwick admired the old man's great wit.

"I say, Chadwick, I wandered down here to speak with you a bit, and I need to find a Holmes book or two to read for the holidays. Please, I ask for your recommendation. I am sure you can pick me out a new adventure. I have had a bit of a yearning to read another story or two about the great detective, you know, before I cannot enjoy them anymore."

Chadwick nodded and said, "Of course, John, of course, we will pick one or two out for you."

"Good, good, but I have a threefold reason for chatting. I of course, would like to wish you a happy Christmas and a wonderful new year. Second, to pick up a book, and last of all, I know you are a great reader, a bit of a literary critic, and I do require your professional assistance. I would enjoy, dear Chadwick, when you have a bit of time to read a manuscript for me, and give the writer a few tips and some input. I have read it, and I dare say, even though I might be a bit partial to the creator of the material, I think the author has some great potential. If you would be so kind as to bring me my coat, Chadwick, I will give you the papers."

Mr. Alcott motioned for Chadwick to hand him his coat from the hook, and Chadwick stood up and walked over to the coat hook. He picked the coat off the hook, walked back, and handed the coat to Mr. Alcott.

Mr. Alcott dug around in the pockets, (it was then that you could clearly see his short arm) picked out a folded stack of papers, and he placed them in his lap.

"Thank you, old boy," Mr. Alcott said while studying the papers in his hands.

"Sure, sure, John," Chadwick said as he hung the coat back up on the hook. "Happy Christmas to you and your family John, and a blessed new year my old friend," Chadwick said as he rejoined Mr. Alcott in a chair next to him.

"Thank you, Chadwick. I had the author make a photocopy of the original manuscript for me. It is handwritten, but his writing is very easy to read. He mostly prints rather than writes in an overhand. I would like your opinion of the work, and maybe, if you think it is worthwhile, then perhaps, some encouragement. You see . . . the author is my grandson, Paul John Henson."

"Oh, my really, your grandson, Paul." Chadwick was a bit surprised as he reached out and took the manuscript copy from Mr. Alcott.

"The Time Bomb in The Cupboard," Chadwick said aloud as he glanced at the papers.

"Yes, it is humorous fiction. It seems as if the young man has inherited a good bit of dry humor from his English side, but in actuality, he is telling a story of an actual event here in the old neighborhood. It is a Christmas tale, about accompanying his best friend's family, in order to cut down Christmas trees in rural New Jersey. It is about that lad, Harry M. Redmond Jr. and the Redmond family."

"Oh, my goodness! The Redmond family! Now, they are quite a colorful bunch," Chadwick piped up when Mr. Alcott mentioned the Redmond family.

Everyone in the old neighborhood knew the Redmond family; they lived about three city blocks from Chadwick's store on John Street, over the border in the borough of Haledon. They were a legendary, fun-loving family who lived life to the fullest, with wild picnics in the summer, and wild parties at all times of the year. Chadwick continued to glance at the manuscript in his hands, reading a few lines here and there while Mr. Alcott watched him.

He chuckled outright once or twice at what he had read, looked up at Mr. Alcott and said, "I would be delighted to read this. I have to say that I can see his humor here in some lines right away. It is quite stirring to think that someone is going to chronicle past stories and adventures from this wonderful, old, neighborhood. What we have here crammed into a few city blocks is so special, John. I wonder what will happen to it when change inevitably comes. I was just thinking about that the other day, and how I wish that I could write. I tried a few times, but I just do not have the knack for it. I cannot grasp characters or storylines enough to bring them from my mind, to place them down on paper."

Mr. Alcott leaned back in his chair and looked at Chadwick. He moved towards some type of deep thoughts for a moment or two, when he finally said, "Ah yes, Chadwick, but you, my old friend, do know books and writer's styles better than any man that I have ever met, and a good story is something that does indeed stir your soul. I consider you a critic and expert on writing, and I value your opinion. You know, I love and hold all my grandchildren close to my heart, but there is something different about Paulie boy. He is a complex, and at times conflicted, young man, very kind, and deeply religious too. The funny thing is that you would not be able to detect his religious beliefs because he does not wear them on his sleeve, so to speak, dear Chadwick. The young chap is a deep thinker who notices everything in life in great detail. I wish he would take up the writing. He has a knack for storytelling because of his attention to detail. Once you have time to read the manuscript, I think that you will agree with me. However, Chadwick, all Paulie boy can think about is playing the position of the goalkeeper in hockey. He dreams of being a professional player, much to the chagrin of his dear mum. He comes home battered, cut, bruised, and stitched, but the young man is tough and fearless."

When Mr. Alcott said the words, "tough and fearless," Chadwick laughed aloud, and tapped his old friend's legs in recognition. "Well, even in my tiny, isolated world, I have heard the word on the street that Paul is quite a good hockey player and with you as his grandfather, and Mr. Henson as his father, well, I do not think any other personality traits would be an option!"

"I thank you for the thought, but I cannot help but think that as good a player as he is, there is something else in his future other than hockey, he seems as if he will influence people in his life, but eh, time will tell. Say, while I browse and wait for your suggestion for a book to touch my heart, this Christmas of some story about Baker Street's most famous resident, perhaps a spot of tea would taste good. Eh? After all, sleep is a bit overrated." Mr. Alcott rose from his chair, smiled, and moved towards the rows of books.

"I will put a teapot on, John. Please browse and enjoy. I will be right back."

The rest of the afternoon, the two friends spent lost in various adventures on Baker Street, as well as a few adventures and memories of the equally famous, Belmont Avenue in Paterson, New Jersey.

Chapter 3

A Mean-Spirited Visit

Christmas Day grew closer, and much to Chadwick's surprise, Ye Olde Book Shoppe did a good bit of business here and there. Since the schools were discharging for a holiday break, and there were no immediate needs for textbook turnover, the store traffic surprised Chadwick a bit. He never ran advertisements; he only relied on the store being in the same place for close to fifty years, and word of mouth to generate sales. On an early Friday afternoon, Chadwick was stocking shelves, and moving some of his inventory around, when the front door to the store opened, and inside the store walked Mr. Roland A. Profitt.

Chadwick sighed, and he frowned a bit. Mr. Profitt was the last person, he wanted to see today, or in fact, on any day.

"Well, good afternoon Chadwick. I see that you are not very happy to see me," Mr. Profitt said, while he looked over towards Chadwick.

Chadwick did not answer him. He shook his head and gathered the books he was working on, and carried them over to the counter.

Roland A. Profitt was the youngest in a long line of men in the Profitt family. Everyone knew of, or heard of, the Profitt family throughout the city of Paterson, in fact, even beyond. They were extremely wealthy, having made a great deal of money in the printing business, the dye business, and they had briefly dabbled in the silk and lace business. Recently, Chadwick had heard they had sold some of the silk and lace mills to Mr. Dalby. Most of the

Profitt family members were obnoxious, but Roland was the worse of the bunch. He had recently returned to the area and the family businesses, after working in New York City, in some type of financial business.

He attended some elite, out-of-state university, where they erased his mind, and filled it with outlandish, fictitious teachings of a false world, taught by professors who never set foot in the real world, and never dreamed there was a place such as Belmont Avenue in Paterson, New Jersey.

He now dabbled in commercial and residential real estate, and he was always seeking to buy the land that Chadwick's store sat upon, as well as the vacant lot next door to the bookstore. One of Roland's printing factories sat adjacent to Chadwick's property between Belmont Avenue and the end of Tilted Hill, and Roland was seeking to expand the factory building, as well as provide additional parking for his employees.

Roland was short, dark featured, with perfectly groomed black hair. He was very lean in his build, nervous, paranoid, and obnoxious. He imagined every single person was out to steal money from him, or take advantage of him in some way, shape, or form, when it actually was the opposite situation. Chadwick surmised that he was an avid fan of the famous *Dark Secrets* magazine, and the periodical's endless conspiracy theories, and covert plans, of evil, shadowy figures lurking around every dark corner of the world, which filled the magazine's pages.

He was around his late thirties in age, just a few years younger than Chadwick was, with a pretty wife, some small children, a gorgeous house on the eastside of Paterson, he drove a nice car and he had everything a man could ask for and desire.

On the other hand. Did Roland really have it all?

Every conversation, and virtually every word from

Roland, was condescending, and laced with intricate questions, and carefully worded traps to lure you into speaking a mistaken word or two, in which Roland could pounce upon, in order to question you some more. It was a very uncomfortable experience when you spoke with him because he quickly grew on your nerves.

All he thought about was business and money. It was never any other type of conversation with this chap. He also possessed the most annoying habit of prefacing almost every sentence in a conversation with an abrupt, and loudly pronounced, "Well," all in an effort of over emphasizing the dramatic impact of every sentence. He also constantly utilized annoying buzzwords in all of his sentences, such as, "I am seeking solutions, I have expectations, and I purchase answers, not excuses."

It was exhausting to converse with him. Roland also was under the constant delusion that everyone in the entire world worked for, or answered to, him.

It was his "expectation!"

Chadwick knew this conversation was not going to be a pleasant inquiry into a book purchase.

Roland approached the front counter and immediately started his usual drivel, "Well . . . it is my expectation that you take time to hear my latest offer for this store, as well as the vacant land beside here. After all, I am offering a solution to your troubles due to a profound and desperate lack of retail business, Mr. Ripplewood Jr."

"I am fine, thank you for asking, Mr. Profitt," Chadwick answered him with a rather curt throwback aimed at Roland's lack of even some vain effort at a courteous discussion.

"I do not have any troubles due to a profound lack of business, Roland. That is some type of false perception of reality to you, in order to justify your visit here today."

"Well . . . please do not take this as blunt, but I find that hard to believe. There is never a soul in this store and the neighborhood has changed dramatically over the past few years. Besides, you offer no parking, and I am very certain, the big mall type stores out on the highway offer much improved solutions for purchasing books than your old, dusty, store here does."

"I am busy right now grading some books, Mr. Profitt, and despite whatever offer you are going to come up with today, I am just not interested. This is the same answer that I have given to you the last twenty or thirty times you have offered me a real estate deal."

"Well . . . you do realize, Chadwick, that you are holding up a perfectly natural progression of turnover in this neighborhood, and that you are adversely affecting my business. The solution that I require is land to expand, and this old neighborhood will continue to deteriorate to the point where residential and retail properties will no longer be viable solutions here. Therefore, your retail operation, and small apartment here, will be trapped inside an industrial and decayed urban paradigm, and you will regret the day you rejected my solution, as well as my generous monetary offer."

"I have no idea of what you are speaking of, Roland. Now, if you have no further need for books, or interest in making a purchase, I dare say, I will bid you good afternoon, and I will return to my work."

Mr. Roland A. Profitt now became visibly upset with Chadwick, for not even entertaining any discussion of a prospective sale, or even any inquiry, as to the figure that Roland intended to offer.

"Well . . . are you not even interested in my supremely generous offer of twenty-five thousand dollars for this rundown store, with a horrid, cramped apartment, and a vacant, rat-infested, city lot, Chadwick?"

Chadwick B. Ripplewood Jr. was a kind and patient man and not known for his temper or any outbursts.

Yet, in this world, every man has a breaking point.

Chadwick placed the books on the counter. He softly withheld his emotions while carefully explaining, "For what I truly hope is the last time, Roland, I do not care what amount of money you have to offer, the land, store and residence, are not for sale. Now, good day, sir."

"Well . . . then, I will consider your palpable, outward display of ignorance to be a sign of your poor business skills. The trouble with you, Chadwick, is that you are lost in a maze of the past. All these silly, old, dusty books are symbols of a useless enterprise, a worthless waste of time. Moreover, you, Ripplewood Jr. are a fool, and a hopeless, clueless dreamer! You are lost in printed words on bound pages and clinging to false hopes and dream worlds, of what this old neighborhood used to be, as opposed to what it is now. Ha! Open your eyes! The heyday is now long since gone! How sad, Ripplewood Jr., trapped forever, here in this dumpy, old, store, and stuck on pitiful Belmont Avenue, clinging to a false hope of the return of a girlfriend who has long ago forgotten who you are! Yes! We all know the story. The truth is on the street as to why you continue to remain here."

Mr. Profitt pointed his finger angrily towards Chadwick and continued his "little, rich boy," temper tantrums.

"Well . . . she is not coming back, and I offer you a solution, an escape from this way of life, and you could take all the money, retire somewhere, and live rather comfortably. Instead, you choose to dream and fritter away your life in and amongst dusty, old dreams and wasting your years, reading words from other clueless dreamers who could only write them on pages! Real men, such as what I am, we act upon our dreams and hopes. We do not just write about them, or dream endlessly!"

That was it!

Chadwick B. Ripplewood Jr. reached his breaking point! He looked up and stared out at the pompous and pretentious young man, slowly walked around to the front of the counter, and leaned on the front of it. Only a few feet separated the two men. It appeared for just a moment or two that Roland A. Profitt thought that Chadwick was resorting to a physical confrontation to even the score for his remarks, and his mean-spirited verbal attack.

Roland took a step or two backwards, perhaps, to be on the safer side.

Chadwick folded his arms across his chest and calmly spoke, "Please do not interpret my kindness for weakness, Mr. Profitt. However, you sir, are an idiot. You are a twisted, shallow minded, evil wreckage of a young man, whose money has blinded him to life, and to human emotions. And, at all times of the year, how dare you come in here, into my own store at Christmas time, or for that matter, at any time, to try to strong arm me by attacking my lifestyle and occupation."

"Oh, please . . . Ripplewood Jr.! Since you are lost in, a false world let me guess, now, I am a character in your favorite Christmas book. An evil miser who wreaks havoc upon the holiday, and then he has ghosts come floating by at night in my mansion, and they convince me to change my so-called terrible ways. Better yet, how many weak storylines in those dull books upon those shelves have the same tired, old storylines of the mean, wealthy, land baron inflicting terror upon poor families, so he can steal and then bulldoze their hapless lands? Please, Chadwick! I am a businessman and deal with real life!"

Chadwick was enraged now, and he pointed his finger abruptly at him, while Roland continued backing away from Chadwick in fear.

Chadwick almost shouted at him, "To answer your question, Roland. Yes, an awful lot of books do have that storyline. They have that common storyline because throughout history there were malcontents such as you around. And, I can only hope for three ghosts to visit you tonight. You spoiled little brat! You were handed silver spoons plated with gold. Now you will need to shut up, and listen to my side of the story. I do not care about your money, or any of your offers, or whatever, else you want to wave in my face. When the time comes, this glorious old store will fade away into history, but only I will decide when that time will be! I have all I need right now. I am richer in life than you could ever wish to be, as are all the folks you belittle in this neighborhood. All you want this land for is to enlarge your factory, provide free parking, and nearby jobs for poor folks, who rather not take the bus into downtown or beyond. They will agree to take your low-paying jobs, therefore maximizing your profits, and then you will sell the factory, right before you know that a downturn is coming, and move on towards the next deal."

Chadwick turned, and he pointed at the rows upon rows of books in the store shelves as he continued his speech.

"The dusty, dull books, as you call them, that surround us have brought me to every corner of the globe and beyond. I have known adventures, mystery, romance, despair, history, happiness, humor, war, pride, prejudice, hope, joy, and met some of the world's most colorful and memorable people. Inside these books are the words that started and ended wars, gave the world the word of God, proclaimed freedom, and they have spread joy throughout the world. What I have learned from reading those dusty, dull, books are worth a million of your useless education. I know facts, history, and events better than most history professors do. In addition, as far as this wonderful, old, neighborhood goes, it will live on forever more, until the end of time. Just to burn your little ass, it will still be here, despite your efforts at turning it into a bulldozed maze of money making for you and your family. Yes indeed, it may change. The people will die, and move away, with new folks to replace them. However, I assure you that it will live not only in memories, but in stories such as this one is."

Chadwick reached around to his drawer on the backside of the counter, and pulled out the manuscript given to him a few weeks ago by Mr. Alcott. He waved it in the air in front of Roland A. Profitt and continued his sharp and angry rebuttal.

"A young, aspiring writer, a . . . storyteller . . . who chose to record the people, events, and history of this wonderful, old place. He records all of it, Roland, so that years from now, he will have enriched readers' lives with stories that allow them, no matter where they are, to meet people such as Harry M. Redmond Jr., Mr. Porter, Ronzo Boatmann, the old man, and others."

Chadwick waved his hands and arms out towards the front of the store, displaying the unity of the neighborhood in front of it.

He then continued, "Then they, will all know that such colorful and wonderful people do exist in this world! And, the young man who wrote this, I can assure you, he is not a clueless dreamer who will not act upon his hopes and dreams, or fritter away his life. It may not look like much to you, Roland A. Profitt, but the folks in these four or five city blocks, are richer than all of the Profitt families put together are! It does not show in their bank accounts, no, no, no, it shows in their hearts. Now, good day, and by the way, my personal life is indeed none of your business. If a worthless dope such as you, can slightly comprehend the meaning of the holiday . . . then, I do wish you a happy Christmas. Please, do not let the front door hit you in your sorry ass on the way out."

Roland frowned and stammered a bit. He did not know how to respond to the tongue-lashing that Chadwick had just given him.

After floundering nervously, he finally said, "Well . . . I will report this poor business negotiating tactic to my uncle. We will see if there is an angle for a potential rezoning of this entire block with the city to void any retail operations. Then, we will pursue possible options of. . .."

"GOOD DAY, MR. PROFITT! I do not need to remind you that you have already tried that tactic two years ago!"

Upon seeing the anger in Chadwick's face, and knowing that he lost the battle, Roland A. Profitt turned and exited the front door.

He did indeed; scoot a bit to the side to make sure that the door did not hit him in his sorry ass on the way out of the store.

Chapter 4

A Christmas Day in 1976

It might have been the disturbing visit from Roland A. Profitt, which had stirred Chadwick's soul and mind, but Chadwick suddenly found himself uneasy in his spirit and his thoughts of his future. After all, no matter how much in your heart you knew that Roland was wrong in voicing his treacherous comments, you could not overlook the inevitable fact that change was coming. Reluctantly, that evening as Chadwick sat alone in his apartment with some soft Christmas music from his favorite Harvey Crooner album (the recording was indeed, *A Happy, Happy Christmas,* which was a favorite of many folks) playing on an old turntable, he knew he needed to prepare for the future. He knew he had reached the crossroads of his life. He was not becoming any younger, and time marched onward.

The next morning, he once more, just as he did a few years ago, placed an advertisement in the same New York City newspaper for the negotiation and eventual sale of the same rare book. He was not quite sure what the motivation was; it was a strange feeling that was inside of him these past couple of days. He could not figure it out as to what was stirring his spirit.

This time, Chadwick felt it was indeed time to prepare to move on now, raise some money, and acknowledge the trains of life that were rolling down the railroad tracks. Eventually, the trains will make the station and the journey will end.

On the morning of 23 December 1976, the telephone rang in Ye Olde Book Shoppe. Chadwick, upon answering the call, found it amazing that it was the same gentleman calling that he had spoken to, when negotiating the original deal on the book, at the time right before Grace Pickering had left for England.

Chadwick humbly explained that he never would have thought to call him since so many years had passed from the original negotiations. The two men chatted for a long time, and they worked out the details of a sale. They also worked out an agreeable price based upon a final inspection of the grading of the condition of the book. The gentleman advised Chadwick that his overseas investor was preparing a visit to the states for the holidays, and would close the deal on the book in person at Chadwick's store.

The two men made an appointment for Christmas Eve at ten in the morning to complete the deal and the transaction.

Christmas Eve found Chadwick working in his bookstore, selling a few books for gifts here and there. Not too many books, but just a few. He was content with his decision, and Chadwick knew the path he now had to take. He needed to plan now. The future was here, and the past was long since gone.

A light snow had started at daybreak, and it had grown in intensity as the morning marched on. Chadwick watched as Belmont Avenue, in front of his store, slowly turned white. Around ten o'clock in the morning, Chadwick received a telephone call from the representative of the book investor, explaining how the poor weather had delayed flights into Newark Airport. Chadwick understood. In fact, he had anticipated a delay. He advised the gentleman that he had no plans until tonight, when he would attend Christmas Eve candlelight church services at eleven o'clock. The telephone call ended with a waiting game. There was not too much that you could do to argue with a snowstorm.

The day dwindled down. Chadwick's dusty, old Christmas tree sparkled in the store window, the train chugged endlessly around the tracks; he shoveled the sidewalk in front of his store, cleared the steps of snow, and no further customers came in.

Christmas Eve came upon the city of Paterson, New Jersey, once more. A city snowplow rolled up the road, with the familiar sound of the blade pushing snow along the roadway. The clack, clack, clack, of the steel snow chains on the number fourteen city bus that rolled up and down Belmont Avenue in the snow-covered streets, kept Chadwick B. Ripplewood Jr. company. He could almost tell time by the passing of the bus.

He now sat alone in his store, staring in silence at the glow of his Christmas tree, watching the little train chug endlessly around the same old circle. He sat there while listening to A.M. radio station WPAT in downtown Paterson; turn over their playlist to a program of all Christmas music for thirty-six hours straight.

He glanced at the clock as the hour hand passed three in the afternoon, and he knew the weather was creating tough sledding for the investor. He planned today to close the store at four in the afternoon. Chadwick would then sit in his store, at the little table set in front of the rows of books, to once again read, *A Christmas Carol.* He would set out some cheese, sip some white wine, light some candles, and enjoy the magical tale of a miserly, old curmudgeon and ghosts.

The tradition needed to continue.

At four in the afternoon, Chadwick turned over the "OPEN" sign in the front door of the store to "CLOSED" and he decided to keep the small Christmas display turned on in the store window. He slowly made his way to the backroom to climb the wooden hill to his apartment. He would head to his kitchen to follow his plan to prepare his wine and cheese snack as a prelude to his reading. A few steps into the climb, Chadwick suddenly heard a loud knock at the door of the store.

"Oh my! The investor has finally made it," Chadwick exclaimed as he turned back down the stairs and made his way through the store.

He did not turn any lights on in the dark store, but made his way via the glow of the lights on the Christmas tree. Through the front store glass and the whipping snow, he could see a person, dressed in a hat and a heavy overcoat and a person, who was standing on the front steps to the store. The person bent over in a vain attempt to shield their body from the snow and cold. Chadwick noticed a city taxicab pull away from the curb, which he surmised had just dropped the person off at the entrance to his store.

"Please, come in out of the weather. Please! The snow has made for a wonderful Christmas backdrop. However, it also wreaks havoc upon any travel," Chadwick was shouting out to the person standing outside while he turned the lock on the door and flung it open.

He was not paying much, if any, attention to the features of the person who was standing in front of his store. His only goal was to allow the poor soul out of the blinding and fierce weather.

When the person stepped in amongst flying snowflakes and wind-driven cold and looked at Chadwick, it was as if his heart rose out of his chest, and his eyes fell out of their sockets.

You see, standing in front of him was Ms. Grace Pickering!

Oh my! It was Ms. Grace Pickering!

Chadwick stepped back in shock. He stumbled a bit and held onto a display of books near the front door to stop him from toppling over. He was unable to speak; he was unable to stand because the poor man had become overwhelmed by the pure emotions of the moment!

That wonderful voice and soft English accent filled the

air once more.

"Hello, Chadwick. I have come to inquire as to the status of a certain book that you have for sale. I have also come to inquire as to if your heart and your mind are still open to hear my sincere apologies for being wayward for so long. And to see . . . if you will accept my apology and hear loud and very clearly, how much I now know that I love you dear, Chadwick B. Ripplewood Jr.," Grace softly spoke while she stood in the front of the store, with tears mixed in with Christmas Eve snowflakes running down her cheeks, and dripping upon the floor.

"Grace! Oh Lord, Grace Pickering! My—my—my—I am at a loss for words. This is like some story in a book that I know I have read at one time, but I cannot recall what the characters said to each other. The Christmas magic has not only overwhelmed me, but it also has taken over my soul! Am I dreaming, or are you really here? It seems as if it is magic that has brought you here, my dear Grace."

Chadwick was still stumbling over his words, but his heart was so full of joy at the sight of his beloved Grace that he could not contain his elation.

The two of them embraced, and shared a kiss of long, lost years, and lonely, days and nights apart.

Grace removed her hat and coat, and Chadwick hung them up on the coat hook near the front door. The two of them hugged, kissed, and embraced once again.

Chadwick finally managed to speak amongst some powerful emotions, "Of course Grace, of course, I still love you! I cannot ever fully explain to you, all the joy in my heart right now, all those lonely days, dreaming of where you were, and when, and if, you would return."

Chadwick looked away; he did not desire for Grace to see the tears forming in his eyes.

He composed himself and said, "I lost contact with you. I lost hope, and I lost a part of myself."

"Shhh, my dear Chadwick, it is over now. I am here with

you to stay if you still will have me."

"Yes! Yes! Grace, but I am so confused. A man called, we worked out a deal, and he then sent an investor. How do you know about the book?"

Grace led Chadwick gently by his hand, and they both sat down at the table opposite one another.

"I understand your confusion, Chadwick. Please, before you hear my story, please know that I will fully understand if you turn me away despite your statement of love and joy of my return."

"Oh, Grace . . . I would never. . .."

"Please, Chadwick, I am the one who has been confused and I owe you, my dear man, the entire story. Please, listen first. . .."

Grace held her hands over Chadwick's as the two of them clenched each other's hands on top of the table. Chadwick nodded to indicate that he would listen, and he handed Grace a handkerchief to dry her eyes from the snow and tears.

She started to speak slowly, "Dear Chadwick, you see . . . the investor interested in your book is my grandfather in England. I am the granddaughter of Wilbert Dalby. Yes! That same, Mr. Dalby—the wealthy person who owns all these mills and lace factories here in Paterson. I only provided you with vague details as to my heritage and relatives because I did not want you to be uncomfortable with a woman from the so-called uppity or gentry side of town! As a very young girl, growing up with him and my grandmother, we all read the classic books together. . .." Grace's voice trailed off; she was choking on some emotion.

After stopping, she regained her voice and continued, "I obtained my own interest in books and reading from my grandparents. Wilbert Dalby is an avid reader, somewhat of a historian, and now you know that he has passed his intense interest in classic books and reading onto his granddaughter. My grandfather is a wealthy and somewhat determined man, and he had his heart set upon procuring your rare book. He can be ruthless in business as so many other wealthy businessmen can be at times."

Chadwick laughed gently as his thoughts drifted towards the wonderful and congenial Mr. Roland A. Profitt.

Grace continued, "When my grandfather called me, and advised me that there was a small-time book dealer in Paterson that was selling this rare book that he had sought for so many years, and Grandfather instructed me to purchase it . . . well, I knew it was yours! I also knew from our discussion that day when you proudly showed me your collection, and the obvious hints you provided, what you were planning to do. I panicked. Grandfather was feeling poorly, and I had an excuse to return home to tend to his needs. He had his heart set upon obtaining your book before, and if, he passed away, and please, I hope you understand that I could never allow you to sell him the book. I knew that if I returned to England, you would withdraw the sale of the book, and it turns out that I was correct in my calculation."

Grace gripped Chadwick's hands tighter, and she looked deeply into his eyes.

She continued to explain, "You see, my dear Chadwick, what you may or may not realize, is that book is a large part of your heritage. It is a part of your very soul, a piece of your heart, and to sell it to raise money to buy a silly ring, for a silly woman, who does not need any additional fancy rings, would be a grave error. I fled, rather than deal with the situation. It was ridiculous, it was mean, and it was wrong."

Grace now was once more choked and filled with emotion, and her tears flowed down her cheeks and fell upon the old table.

"Grandfather, made a full recovery, and he is doing rather well right now. I did not know at the time how to deal with a marriage proposal if that was indeed your intent. I knew that Grandfather, Grandmother, and my own parents, would pitch a bit of a fit at the news of such a union between us. They feel that I am a bit of a queen and that I should be seeking some stuffy blue blood to spend my life with forever. Confusion reigned in my mind, dear Chadwick! Therefore, in a self-centered and rather futile hope of forgetting you, I purposely avoided communication with you. When Grandfather once again became aware of the sale of your book, he summoned me here to purchase it. I was filled with horror that you had found another and were planning to marry. I could not bear that thought. I knew that I had to come, beg forgiveness, tell you the entire story, and tell you, how much I love you."

Grace wiped her eyes with the handkerchief, looked down, and then back towards Chadwick.

"I see by your reaction, and knowing your character, that somehow, I have been mistaken. Kissing another woman and professing love to her, while attached to another, is not the Chadwick B. Ripplewood Jr. that I know so well. Therefore, I have made an error of some sort. Chadwick, this is, as if it is a plot from some book that we both have read. I have to say it is so dramatic in nature. Please tell me that you forgive me. Tell me that you understand, and you understand that I do not need rings, or fancy houses, I only need you, Chadwick B. Ripplewood Jr."

Chadwick stirred in his seat. He leaned back a bit, while slowly losing grip with Grace's hands, and he sat as if he was pondering the situation deeply. He then leaned back in his chair, smiled, and gently grasped her hands again.

He spoke proudly, with just a touch of a wry smile upon his face, "I am very sorry to tell you, Ms. Pickering that despite the tremendously long distance that you have traveled through, and fighting this terrible weather, on a holiday evening such as this, well, I have changed my mind. The book is no longer for sale, and the offer of sale is hereby withdrawn."

Grace lost her grip with Chadwick's hands and she sat back, puzzled as to where the conversation was leading.

"I will, however, propose an alternative offer. I was just about to enjoy some white wine, some cheese, light some candles, and engage in my annual Christmas Eve reading of A Christmas Carol. After that, I intended to read once again, a draft manuscript of a humorous, but slightly factual novelette, with a Christmas storyline, in which I fortuitously came upon from a fledging, local author."

Chadwick chuckled a bit, his heritage of inheriting a bit of wry English humor, now was in full swing, "My plans, then included dressing for church, walking the few city blocks in the snow to Cedar Cliff United Methodist Church, and attend a Christmas Eve candlelight worship service. I would be very excited if you decided to join me in this evening's plans. If I may be so bold as to ask you to stay the night, and then we can share Christmas Day together. I do not have a gift for you other than myself, but I do know where we can obtain a good book or two to read tomorrow, and on Boxing Day, and beyond, in fact, forever."

Grace smiled widely, and her eyes sparkled. She grasped Chadwick's hands tightly as she softly whispered, "I will be delighted, and I joyfully accept your alternative offer. I assure you that there are no hard feelings on the withdrawing of the first offer. I feel the second one is a far superior one indeed!"

There in the quiet of the old store, sitting at an old wooden table, with Christmas music as a backdrop, and snow gently falling outside, Ms. Grace Pickering and the suddenly, very wealthy, Mr. Chadwick B. Ripplewood Jr., added a page or two, or three, to their own book.

Chapter Five

The Old Neighborhood Returns

Time and change finally did catch up with the old neighborhood, as well as with Ye Olde Book Shoppe. When the inevitable time finally arrived to close the store, sell the property, and the vacant land, it was a deal to relish for Chadwick B. Ripplewood Jr. and Mrs. Ripplewood Jr. It turns out that Mr. Roland A. Profitt was not as keen a businessperson as the rest of his family, and his dye and printing operation fell apart, and eventually closed.

He, of course, blamed it on Chadwick B. Ripplewood Jr. and his lack of cooperation in obtaining an agreement to sell Roland A. Profitt the land, in which he required for expansion of his factory and mill. Chadwick and others felt it was fate and was a result of Roland's poor attitude catching up with him.

Perhaps, it was the old adage of "You reap what you have sowed" type of karma.

The factory sat abandoned for quite a bit of time. It sat until a certain powerful New Jersey state senator named William T. Hobnobber, approached Chadwick and his wife, about selling their property to allow for proper expansion of the former Profitt factory and mill. Senator Hobnobber was head of an urban renewal project in the New Jersey state senate to restore old neighborhoods, fight back on urban decay, and bring jobs to people who desperately required them.

In an extreme case of irony, the businessman who purchased the entire package including the Ripplewood's building and vacant land was none other than the now famous, Mr. Harry M. Redmond Jr.!

Mr. Redmond had returned a wealthy man to New Jersey after some time away, and he required a factory to produce quirky gadgets he invented, as well as find a location for his custom metal fabrication and welding enterprise.

Mr. Redmond wanted nothing more than to bring his new operation back to the old neighborhood, to a location only three or four city blocks away from where he grew up.

Part of the agreement included the preservation of the former store and dwelling. The bombastic, engaging, and gregarious, Mr. Redmond proudly told Chadwick and his wife that he would not bulldoze or remove the building. Mr. Redmond planned instead to turn the property into his own private company offices. He insisted to Chadwick B. Ripplewood Jr. that it would not be any other way.

And, as they tend to say in the old neighborhood, even to this day, that Mr. Harry M. Redmond Jr. could sell ice to an Eskimo!

It was wonderful; a remarkable tie back to the old neighborhood and Roland A. Profitt once more was wrong in his mistaken prediction for the old neighborhood.

It was a few weeks before Christmas in the year 2002, and Chadwick B. Ripplewood Jr. was browsing with his wife in a large, "big box" bookstore at a shopping mall in lower New York State. The shopping mall was not very far away from the house, in which Grace and Chadwick had retired to a few years earlier, but it was indeed a good bit of distance away from Belmont Avenue.

In a great twist of irony, this was just the type of store that had encroached upon Ye Olde Book Shoppe so many years ago, when the tide turned on "mom and pop" type shops and stores.

The couple strode hand in hand, up and down the aisles, killing time in what was still their favorite pastime.

Ah, yes, just the smell of the books inspired them!

There, very close to the front door of the store, was a

book display with a brightly colored sign proudly displaying, "New Releases, Christmas Stories" in large letters.

As Chadwick stopped in front of the display to scan over the books, his eyes grew wide as a certain book caught his eye. He eagerly reached down and grabbed the book while smiling widely and laughing aloud.

"Why Grace! Look! The Time Bomb in The Cupboard and Other Adventures of Harry and Paul!"

"Oh, Chadwick! I see! It is marvelous indeed! I guess he eventually did take your advice after all."

"Yes, yes, yes. I guess, he did," Chadwick mumbled as he opened the pages, and scanned the words. He then began to read the words aloud to his wife, "My best buddy growing up was Harry M. Redmond Junior. Even as a little kid and as a teenager, he was loud, bombastic, friendly, and outgoing. He had a mischievous side, but for the most part, he stayed out of trouble. He was a great friend to hang with; no one was more fun. Harry and his family were the same. They all were happy, gregarious, and over the top in everything, they did. There was no middle road with any of the Redmonds. There was nothing on Earth that he and his family liked better than a party, a holiday, or any kind of big shindig that you could ever imagine."

Chadwick looked at Grace and smiled, while he flipped the pages to the back of the book, and read the words to himself as his wife watched, and she smiled at her husband's obvious excitement.

Chadwick then said, "Oh my, Grace, listen to this! We knew that in the world of Harry and Paul, there would be another adventure right around the corner. There always will be, you see Harry and Paul adventures never really end. The years may pass, but they go on forever, as long as there are memories, dreams to dream, fun-loving people who enjoy life and care for one another in special ways, stories to tell, roads to travel, music to hear, dances to dance, and love to give. They go on and on until the end of all time."

Chadwick closed the book, and tears filled his eyes as his wife hugged him.

"Please, dear, let's buy a number of copies and send them as gifts this year. I cannot wait to read the entire book. The author has added a number of stories to the original manuscript. We can even look up an address for a certain Mr. Roland A. Profitt and send him a copy. I would love to see the look on his smug, little face. I want him to know the old neighborhood will never fade . . . it will . . . just as I told him, truly exist in some way, now until the end of all time."

THE END

Epilogue

The old northern New Jersey neighborhood along Belmont Avenue, between North 9th Street, up Burhans Avenue, over to Roe Street, back over to Lee Avenue, and ending around Henry Street, or thereabouts in Paterson, and Haledon, New Jersey, is a very special place on this good earth.

In addition, the people who lived there in the 1960s, 70s, and 80s were very special too. Years ago, everyone worked together, bonded, and the residents were tough and determined, yet kind and helpful.

Nowadays, it is very difficult to tell. . ..

On special days, such as Christmas Day, extra joy echoed across the old neighborhood, and church bells rang out symbolic hope into every corner of the city's blocks. People heard them and stopped, thought about it, and took it all in, the joy of the bells ringing in their ears, a reminder, and a broadcast of hope, joy, and peace for everyone.

No matter how far some original residents travel in their own lives, they will always bring a piece of the old neighborhood with them. Christmas, Easter, Thanksgiving, and everyday memories tucked away forever, no matter where they are.

We can only hope they continue to tell stories of those times since it would be shameful to lose them.

In the quiet still of a Christmas night on Belmont Avenue in Paterson, and Haledon, New Jersey, when the city buses no longer run and the people are all sleeping, you can still hear it. It starts very low, and then rises up in volume, until it fills your very soul. The laughter, the voices of the past, the joy, the hope, the church bells of Cedar Cliff United Methodist and Saint Paul's Church ringing in unison, the adventures and memories of everyone. It lives on forever.

May the joy and hope of Christmas Day ring out forever more! We pray that everyone continues to hear the peal of the church bells of the old neighborhood, if not in their ears, then in their hearts, no matter where they are on the face of God's great creation.

Bonus Story

The Last Roll on Old Number 95

The Last Roll on Old Number 95

While he walked the length of the train, he checked all the nooks and crannies in each of the cars, and he had made a last safety check. It was difficult for Mr. Stanley Ellsworth to think this was his last trip. His last roll on the old number Ninety-Five train. It began on a whim. He was only twenty-two years of age; his wife was pregnant with their first child and times were difficult. Jobs were scarce. As in almost non-existent. On the advice of a neighbor, Stanley applied to the railroad as a conductor trainee. He gave up his dream of being a lead guitarist and singer in a rock-and-roll band, bid his band mates goodbye and good luck, and hit the rails. He shaved his beard, cut off all of his long hair, pushed the marijuana and alcohol-infused nights of gigs in smoky bars and clubs aside, and took up a new life. He told his wife that he would do this for a few years, until the economy recovered, his guitar skills improved, and he could find a band with some more consistent and reliable gigs. This was a union position; the benefits were amazing, and the pay was decent. Forty-six years later and millions of miles of riding the rails, his old electric guitar and six-string acoustic guitar gathered dust on their carrying cases inside the depths of an upstairs closet in their home. They were not high-quality instruments, but for the money that he had at the time to invest in them; they were not too bad. Could he play a few notes and chords on the instrument if he had to? Perhaps. Stanley always felt as if his singing voice was not the best, not the worst, but not the best. He had not sung a note in years. Not even while driving in his car or while in the shower. He often wondered why that was so. His love of music and a musical career remained a faint dream of his past, and mostly, a lost memory of what seemed as if it was a different life.

Yet, this railroad career had been a wonderful time. In retrospect, Stanley felt as if he made a solid choice, for his family, for his wife and for his stability and his soul.

Stanley had seen it all and experienced it all as he rolled away the miles. All while swaying to the beat of the rail cars rather than a rock-and-roll band, from helping to deliver a baby, to assisting the police in tracking down a wanted criminal, to storms, to breakdowns on the tracks to you name it and Stanley had been through it. He met different persons from every walk of life. From doctors to nurses, to attorneys, to loud-mouthed, brash, horn blowing politicians, to movie stars, to sports stars, to mobsters, to intellects, to hippies and alcoholics and sober people, some priests, some nuns and hellfire and brimstone preachers of the Gospel. You name a person and Stanley had met one of them. One thing for sure, Stanley would always stop and talk with a musician, when they walked onto his train with an instrument. He would stop and talk a little music . . . whether the musician played classical music or jazz, or rock-and-roll, or blues, or otherwise, Stanley always talked music. A musician carrying an instrument case always caught his eye and lit up his mind. It invoked a certain joy in his mind and in his soul.

It had been a long ride in so many ways. Still, he would not trade the forty-six years for anything. Sure, there were awful days, but the fun and the good days outweigh them. Forty-six years had gone by in a blur. In the blink of an eye. The conductors, engineers, and lounge car attendants that he had worked with over the years. My goodness, if he had to, Stanley could name most of them. Describe them too! His memory was incredible. He could do the same for regular train riders too.

Nowadays, his lower back ached, and as a result, he walked a little slumped over at the waist and held onto the safety rails a little more than he used to. His knees ached too and his eyesight was not too sharp. His short hair, long since cut down from the wavy locks of his rock-and-roll years, now mostly disappeared from his head. Just a few tufts of white here and there in tiny wisps remained on his head. Stanley carried a little more weight than he used to; however, because he walked miles upon miles inside the trains and was on his feet all day long, it was not excessive. His wife felt as if he filled out his uniform rather handsomely. His brown eyes were a little cloudy now; the eye doctor wanted to laser cut off some cataracts. Maybe. Now that he had more time. Because of his weak eyesight and the cataracts, Stanley had to study the tickets closely to read them. Even while wearing his eyeglasses. He went from punching tickets with a hole-puncher to scanning them with an electronic gizmo and now, the technology on board the trains made his head spin. It was amazing. At age sixty-eight, he thought he could hang on and retire at seventy, but the pain in his back and knees really caught up with him during the past summer. One day in late September, his wife took him out to dinner and over drinks and a fine meal, she told him her thoughts; it was time to ride the rails for the last time. They had enough money; they wanted to do some things together while their health was reasonably good and enjoy life. His pension was outstanding, the benefits would still kick in, and there really was no reason to keep working. It was more of Stanley's spirit and his love of trains that kept him rolling along and his wife knew that he would miss that part of his life, but it was time. Yet, in the back of Stanley's mind, he wondered exactly what he would do in retirement. No more miles, no more crazy schedules. No more train stations, or late nights and early mornings. Honestly, even though Stanley knew that they were heading north on a set of rails that he already had ridden on countless times, Stanley felt as if his last destination was not very clear.

Now, it was Christmas Eve and time for the final ride. Stanley went from an aspiring rock-and-roll star to an old train conductor in the blink of an eye. The railroad had honored Stanley with a retirement dinner and ceremony a few days earlier, and now, all he had left was one last roll from Richmond, Virginia to New Haven, Connecticut. His shift would end at New Haven, although the train would continue to roll to Boston. Stanley would get off at Union Station, turn in his gear, fill in the logs, punch his last time clock ticket and head for his car and ride back home to their house in Newington, Connecticut. One last roll on train number Ninety-Five. The railroad allowed him to keep his railroad issued pocket watch that hung on his vest from a chain. Just as it had hung there for these forty-six years. Management also allowed Stanley to keep his conductor's hat. Last night, in the hotel room, Stanley polished the brass on his watch until it gleamed. He also polished the bill on his conductor's hat and the train badge on the front of it, and he polished his boots until he could see his face in them. Most, if not all the management personnel of train operations that Stanley knew and worked with and grew up with, now had all long since retired, and sometimes, passed away, but the present-day management realized his commitment to the job and his love of trains. It meant a great deal to Stanley to keep those items.

A light snow was falling, and even though the temperature plummeted to below freezing in Richmond and they received sporadic but sometimes substantial snowfalls in central Virginia; snow in Richmond always caused panic. Stanley knew the passengers would arrive on the train a little flustered from the travel to the train station through what they perceived to be a blizzard. An obstacle on a frantic day of travel home to see loved ones. Perhaps they were journeying to their own homes or visiting relatives, loved ones and friends for Christmas. Perhaps, they were traveling to where they used to live. Stanley would learn a few destinations as he worked the train from the persons who wanted to share some stories, he would surmise the rest from his experience. A quick glance at their luggage, their companions or solo riders, or their attire, and Stanley could determine their destinations and the stories behind them. A lifetime of working this job provided you with special skills. If he did not have all the facts on his side, then Stanley would create stories in his mind. Oh my! The stories that the old train conductor could tell!

For Stanley, the snowfall on a train ride on Christmas Eve, especially on his last ride, was a picture-perfect setting. He could think of no other weather to arrive from Heaven to say his goodbyes to. When Stanley leaned out of the train door of the business class car and a few flakes of snow hit his face, a wide smile broke across his face. He looked into the lights hovering above the walkway and squinted in the darkness to admire the fine snowflakes, slowly drifting down and filtering through the lights. Perfect.

His old eyes scanned the walkway for passengers. The

old conductor walked down the steps and stood on the walkway as the announcements came over the speaker system for boarding of train number Ninety-Five.

A few snowflakes landed on the bill of his train conductor's hat and clung there. Stanley plucked his watch from his belt, flipped it open and checked the time. Five minutes until they rolled north.

This was it.

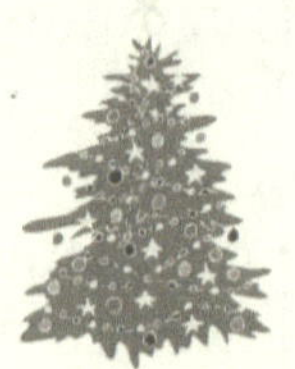

"Tickets!" Stanley called out for what was likely the millionth time plus tenth time that he had called out for tickets. He made his way through the aisles on the trains, checking tickets, scanning the bar codes with his electronic scanner and slipping the ticket stub into the slot above the passenger's seats. He could do this with his eyes closed. Some passengers smiled and said "good morning, or merry Christmas" others remained silent or grumpy or half-asleep. It was five in the morning on Christmas Eve.

Patrick McGuire was his co-conductor on this roll. Stanley was the Head Conductor. Today, Patrick worked from the front of the train to the lounge car, and Stanley took the lounge car to the rear. Unless there was an issue. Patrick was a young fellow, about twenty-five years of age or thereabouts, and he had been on the job for about two years. Stanley liked the young man. He was unassuming and dedicated.

'A rarity amongst his generation,' Stanley thought and felt guilty doing so, but the facts were the facts. In the last three years, he had ridden with about twenty young recruits before Patrick stuck. They were all in and around the same age as Patrick. They all quit for various reasons.

"Too hot, too cold, too many hours, people and all the passengers were all pains-in-the asses and disrespected them."

Nowadays, a perception of disrespect amongst these

young persons was a convenient excuse to bail out when something was too difficult. It provided them with an air of self-importance and pushed their own`lack of fortitude or dedication off on others. Some complained that Stanley was too difficult of a boss; some said that they were away from home too much, and a few said their ears ached at the end of the day because the trains were too noisy. Stanley heard all the excuses and only chuckled. In life, you need to suck it up; not everything is perfect, especially so with employment. Patrick was a lifer. Stanley could tell. He would be proud to hand off his assignments to a trainman such as Patrick was. He would take over and perpetuate the legacy.

The quiet car annoyed Stanley. There was always what he called "Police Officers" in and amongst the passengers. They were pompous businesspersons or stuffy overly educated persons living the high-life from ivory towers, and if a person so much as cleared their throats while they studied their bank accounts and emails on their laptops, they received stern glances or unwarranted reprimands from the police officers guarding the quiet. Now, sometimes, there were dummies who used their cell phones to call Auntie Flo on and yapped up a storm, and those dummies warranted coaching on the rules of the quiet car or ushering into another car, but mostly, the police officers were full of themselves. Luckily, since this was Christmas Eve, the quiet car was mostly empty. No work today meant that most persons wanted to talk or call loved ones or friends on cell phones and enjoy the train ride. Only one stuffy looking grouchy guy sat silently in the quiet car. He was sitting in the window seat, while slowly sipping a coffee and blankly staring at nothing through the darkness as it whipped by the train window next to his seat. Stanley checked his ticket, greeted him with an unanswered, "Good morning," and moved on. His favorite car loomed ahead. Stanley loved working the business class cars. . . ..

"Well, hello there, pretty little gal. Why the tears on Christmas Eve?" Stanley asked as a little girl of about four or five years of age shrunk down in her seat and cuddled into the chest of a stunningly gorgeous woman. Stanley surmised the beautiful woman to be the little girl's mother, and Stanley studied them while he loomed above them, scanning their tickets. There was a striking resemblance between the two of them; therefore, Stanley was sure that his supposition was correct. Mother and daughter. Natural beauties. Gorgeous. Nothing made up or phony. No heavy makeup, no fancy clothes, just warm winter sweaters, jeans and boots. Beautiful. The little girl was a miniature version of Mom. The little girl was adorable, with silky blond hair tucked under a red and green wool cap, with white embroidered reindeer characters woven into the Christmas colors.

"Your daughter?" Stanley asked as the mother nodded and smiled in confirmation.

Stanley handed her ticket back and pushed the button to print out the scan. He looked around, and the car was still rather empty. Stanley had time to scan all the tickets and come back to these passengers. Mother smiled at Stanley's words, his genuine smile, and his warmth. She studied his eyes, his long nose, his immaculate uniform and his cap, and his joyous demeanor, while answering the old conductor's inquiry. The little girl sniffled and used a tissue to wipe away her little tears while the little girl burrowed even deeper into her mother's warmth. Her mother took the tissue, and as mothers often do, she used motherly love to wipe a slightly runny nose due to the passing of the emotions.

"Oh, our precious little, Annie. I suspect that she is so upset because she wanted to stay at home for Christmas. You see . . . her father is overseas on a deployment with the Navy and he will not be home for Christmas. We are traveling to Connecticut to spend Christmas with Grandma and Grandpa."

"Ah, yes, I see," Stanley said while he bent down and smiled at Annie, "missing your daddy, huh?" Annie nodded and remained buried into her mother. "Well, let me first tell you that your daddy is a hero. A special man who loves you and your mother very much and he will stand up to defend all that we have, all that we own and all that we love. I know that you miss him, but be very proud of all that he is. Second, I assure you that today is a special day. This is a special train . . . a Christmas Eve train and you are going to have a wonderful ride and time."

Annie mumbled, "But I don't want to. Santa Claus will not come to me because I am here and going to visit Grandma and Grandpa. I want to be home waiting for Santa with Mommy and Daddy."

"I understand, but please know that . . . Santa Claus knows where you are," Stanley announced while standing up and spreading his arms out far and wide. His balance remained steady even as the train bumped and swayed. His years of navigating the train fine-tuned his steadiness despite the ebb and flow of the train's speed and the twist and turns of the cars upon the rails.

"How?"

Stanley lifted his eyebrows in jest; he playfully looked around and then put his finger to his mouth as if to ask for their silence. He coyly looked around. He then reached into his uniform vest, and in doing so, he pulled out what he knew would be the ace in the deck. "Because of magic. All of life is magical. Sometimes, you need to feel it and open your eyes to see it and most of all to believe in it. I need to tell you a secret. I am Stanley Ellsworth and as Head Conductor on this Christmas Eve train. My job is to know what time it is . . . always."

With those words, he pulled out his amazing brass train pocket watch, dangled it upon the chain hooked to the button on his vest and with his thumb, flipped the lid open. Annie's eyes widened, and she proclaimed, "Wow!"

Stanley had eased hundreds of upset and sniffling children's emotions with this same watch over the years. . .. Annie scooted over closer to study the watch and when Stanley finally saw a hint of a smile on the little girl's face, and she cooed in awe of the watch, the old conductor announced, "Soon it will be time for the train to slow and guess what?"

Annie now was fully captivated.

Stanley checked the time, added a mumbled, "Soon," and flipped the lid closed and he carefully tucked the watch into his vest pocket.

"Santa might just swoop in next to the train and drop off a few presents on the caboose for me, Mr. Stanley Ellsworth, Head Conductor of train number Ninety-Five to deliver for him to children on this train. Annie, trains don't have chimneys."

Annie nodded and smiled, and the tears were gone. Dried up.

"Is this the Polar Express, Mr. Stanley?" Annie asked.

Stanley laughed at her question and a couple across the aisle which were both listening in, and now, held captive by Stanley too, smiled and laughed aloud.

"No," Stanley twisted his mouth up to make a funny face, shook his head, as the little girl's laughter filled the train car, and warmed everyone's hearts, "we are going to Boston, not to the North Pole. However, this Christmas Eve train is even better than the Polar Express is! It is the old number Ninety-Five rolling north on Christmas Eve. I promise that I will be right back. Now, no more tears, right?"

Annie nodded, and Stanley added, "Good. Because we don't want Santa to see tears and sad kiddies and for him to fly right on by the train!" Stanley playfully poked at the air to emphasize his warning. Annie's mother mouthed a "thank you" as Stanley tipped the bill of his conductor's hat and moved on with checking the rest of the tickets. For those passengers close to where Annie and her mother sat and were privy to the conversation, joy filled their hearts. For those that were not . . . Christmas loomed to fill whatever void was in their lives.

In the rear of the train, (sadly, there were no more cabooses on trains these days) Stanley had a small locker where he stashed his luggage, his lunch pail, and in anticipation of some unhappy and some happy children too, the old conductor had bought and wrapped up a few Christmas gifts. There were games, some candy, some candy canes, a few dolls and toy action heroes, and a one little special teddy bear dressed as a train conductor. Yes, Santa Claus would swoop in next to the train and enlist the aid of Stanley Ellsworth and fellow co-workers to help spread a little Christmas joy. It was an act that Stanley pulled off for many, many previous Christmas Eve train rides. Even after these many years, it never wore thin. It only glowed brighter and brighter. Now he would pull it off one more time. The engineer would sound a long blast of the train whistle after a long stop, maybe at Fredericksburg or even at Quantico, and then Stanley would grab the microphone and proclaim a few loud, "Ho, ho, ho" calls and make some thumping noises into the microphone to duplicate reindeers on the roofs of the train cars.

The grumpy passengers in the quiet car would complain. . ..

Stanley and Patrick would hand out the presents, and Marcy in the lounge car would give out free drinks of hot cider, spiked with whiskey for the adults if they so requested it, free hot chocolate drinks for the kiddies, and free Christmas cookies. The parent company of the train operations approved of their little spreading of Christmas joy, but they would not fund it because corporations could not bear to part with a few precious dollars. Duty to the shareholders, you know. . ..

Too bad they would not consider bringing back the cabooses. Cabooses did not generate revenue. Passengers in the seats did.

This was all out of Stanley's own pocket because that was the kind of guy that Stanley Ellsworth was. He gave to the world what he felt that it gave to him, to his wife and to his family. A touch of warmth and love on the last roll was just what he needed to forget for a few moments that this was the last ride for Stanley Ellsworth.

The train and a small part of the world would miss him.

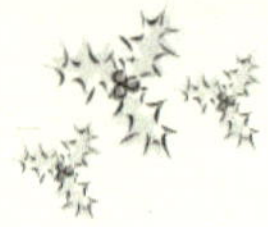

The stop at the train station in Ashland, Virginia, was too short to implement Stanley's plan of Christmas merriment. After a longer stop and after picking up quite a few passengers at the train station in Fredericksburg, Virginia and checking tickets and accommodating their needs, answering questions and taking care of further duties, the crew had a longer run until the next stop. On a long turn where the train could steady out on speed, the engineer blew the train whistle long and hard. The sun was creeping up now, even if you could not see it, but it was light outside the windows of the train and passengers could enjoy the peaceful and serene winter snow scenes outside the windows of the train. The snow was falling harder and steadier now, and beauty abounded. It was the perfect setting, and Stanley grabbed the microphone and performed his best Santa Claus imitation.

"Ho, ho, ho! Merry Christmas everyone!" He followed the joyful broadcast of his melodious voice with some loud thumps into the microphone and all the children onboard the old Ninety-Five train shared in the fun and happiness. Except for the grumpy man in the quiet car and a few of his fellow grouches, because the stock market was open today. Until noon. Stanley needed to check their tickets for the last name of "Scrooge." Stanley gathered the presents into a pillow sack and made his way throughout the cars, spreading joy while Patrick did the same on the other side of the train. He saved a particular teddy bear for a special little girl.

When Stanley finally made his way to where Annie sat with her mother, he reached down deep into the sack and pulled out the present. Stanley blinked back some tears at the joyful face of the little girl and her hands neatly folded in her lap. Anticipation of children at Christmastime is one of life's great joys and the holiday's greatest moments.

"Did you hear Santa Claus, Annie?"

Stanley asked as he pulled out the bear from the depths of the pillowcase.

"I did! I did, Mr. Stanley. Is Santa Claus following the train . . . flying . . . up there?" Annie pointed to the world above the train.

"He sure is. He dropped off this sack of presents until he can arrive at your houses late tonight. He dropped off many presents here for the children onboard. I almost did not catch the sack!" Stanley jumped and feigned a demonstration of how he almost missed the precious airdrop from the big man.

Annie laughed and her mother added, "Great catch, Stanley."

He added with a wink, "I am old, but nimble. Here you go, Annie. Right before he swooped off into the sky, Santa yelled to me that this gift was for you. Merry Christmas."

Annie looked first at her mother, who nodded approval, and then she smiled, mumbled a "thank you" and took the present from Stanley. Wrapping paper tore away in frantic measures and landed in all directions.

"A train conductor teddy! Just like Mr. Stanley is! Thank you, Santa!"

Within seconds, a little girl was hugging the little teddy bear close to her heart. All of her tears were gone and to a certain old train conductor, such a simple moment stole his heart. He wiped at his eyes and was about to turn to retreat to the rear of the train and attempt to hide his tears. When Annie's mother, wiggled out of her seat, she stood and motioned for Stanley to come closer to her.

She gently kissed his cheek and hugged him, whispered, "Thank you. I am Louise Haley. This has been so amazing."

"You are welcome. My pleasure to meet you, Mrs. Haley, and to meet your lovely little daughter too. I am Stanley Ellsworth, Head Conductor of old Ninety-Five. Merry Christmas Eve. Ah, ah . . . please, excuse me, but my duty calls me. . .."

Stanley pointed to the rear of the train. However, Louise knew by the tears rimming his eyes that he really required a private moment or two. She nodded, and Stanley turned on his heels. Slowly, the passengers in the business class car of the old Ninety-Five train clapped their hands together in a round of applause. Then they roared in unison with cheers of support, as the old conductor tipped his hat, smiled, ambled down the main aisle of the train car and disappeared inside of his nook, inside the rear enclave of the car.

There, Stanley took out his handkerchief and, in private, officially wiped away his tears.

"Good job with the Santa Claus visit, guys," the train lounge car attendant, Ms. Marcy Barber said while she leaned on the stainless-steel counter in the lounge car. "We have a bunch of happy kiddies and a few tipsy adults riding the rails. At least, according to the three empty bottles of whiskey and only two remained in the stash. Spiked cider was a big hit." Marcy looked first at Stanley and then at Patrick, and then Marcy added with a smile, "If you mention the word free, it becomes easier to justify a buzz."

The crew was taking a brief break while they rolled north from Quantico, Virginia, to the outskirts of Washington D.C. and the many stops in the capital area. Typically, many passengers got off the train at Washington D.C. and just as many will climb onboard. This is where the train becomes crowded and at Philadelphia, Newark, New Jersey and at Penn Station in New York City it is another mass exodus of travelers. Onward to New Haven and points north, it was always difficult to determine the flow of passengers. Even more so, because it was Christmas Eve. However, chances are the train will empty as they pass by Washington, D.C., New Jersey, and New York City. The snow was falling harder now, and the train plowed ahead. At the Richmond station, maintenance had fitted the locomotive with a snowplow and there were no concerns amongst the crew, with the snow accumulation on the tracks. The railroad radio frequency on the two-way radios clamped to the hips of Marcy, Patrick, and Stanley all chattered with reports from points north and luckily, this was a parched and powdery snow. No ice to cause troubles. The train did shutdown and stop for a long stop in Washington D.C. at the main station downtown. There, maintenance changed the locomotive out to an electric locomotive as they rode the wires the rest of the way to Boston. In addition, there in Washington D.C., the engineer and the crew upfront changed out; however, Patrick, Marcy, and Stanley remained onboard until Union Station in New Haven, Connecticut, when a new conductor crew and lounge car attendant came on board for the rest of the roll north to Boston. All three of them were Nutmeggers, and they were going home for Christmas.

For Stanley, he was going home permanently.

Since the locomotive switched out from diesel fuel to overhead electric from Washington D.C. north, ice on the wires was a concern when it was winter weather. Not today. The cold intensified as they rolled farther north and the ride should be scenic, festive, and trouble free.

"Since we are all off-shift at New Haven, I want to save some of the whiskey for a celebration shot or two to celebrate you, my friend. To celebrate millions of miles and all the joy that you brought along with you on those many journeys. How does it feel to be about halfway from the end of the rails, Stanley?" Marcy asked, as she took a long sip of coffee and studied her boss for an answer to her question.

"Thank you for the celebration shot. That will be nice. I have to say that, well . . . it feels emotional. Very emotional," Stanley admitted with an emphatic shrug of his shoulders. "There is a little girl in the business class car . . . she is missing her dad, who is overseas serving in the Navy, and she was not happy about leaving her home for Christmas. They are heading to Connecticut to spend Christmas with Grandma and Grandpa. All the little girl's angst is because she is so uneasy without her home, her father—it is difficult for her. My goodness, the little gal is so adorable. Maybe she is four years old or five or six, I don't really know. Anyway, I saw her crying and, well," Stanley picked up his coffee and took a sip and then he continued, "it was very emotional. It added to my own emotions. I gave her a teddy bear. Correction . . . Santa Claus gave her a teddy. Dressed as a train conductor."

Patrick nodded and said, "This emotion, ah, where is it coming from, Stanley? Are you happy or sad?"

Stanley downed the rest of his coffee, crumpled the paper container, turned and looked for the trashcan and tossed the container inside.

"Not sure. I am not sure. I think I am numb. All these years, all these miles, all the adventures and the many people I have crossed paths with . . . it all makes my head spin."

Marcy whistled a low whistle and took a sip of her coffee. The lounge car attendant smiled and added, "You just sent a shiver down my spine, Stanley. To think, you have been riding the rails longer than Patrick and I have been alive."

"No doubt, Marcy. That is the crazy thing because looking back . . . it is all a blur now. A blur. In the next few days when the numbness wears off, perhaps, I will feel a huge letdown. Not sure, really. I mean, after the magic of Christmas wears off and the cold of January takes over my life, what exactly will I do?"

"Sure, as hell, not get up at weird and wacky hours," Marcy quickly jumped into the conversation.

With a slow nod, Stanley agreed, and as he lowered his

voice, the old conductor added, "No doubt. Yet, guys, that was part of the magic of it all. In a strange way, the early morning rolls, the sun creeping up over the horizon, the first whistle of the day, the first time that the cars jostled as we moved, somehow, it was and is part of what I think I will miss the most."

Marcy and Patrick did not answer Stanley. It seemed as if both of them did not exactly know what to say. "Well, we best get back at it. A busy stretch is ahead."

Marcy and Patrick nodded, and both of them knew not to comment because they sensed Stanley's emotions. They struggled to imagine, forty-six years and now, when they pull into Union Station in New Haven, Connecticut, it will be the end of the line for Stanley Ellsworth.

New York City was now in the rearview mirror. Not that the train had one. . ..

While they pushed past Westchester County and dabbled with the outskirts of New England, the snowfall was heavy; the air grew colder; the snowplow pushed piles from the track and the train's engineer reduced speed for safety's sake. They would be a little late; however, the train would not be too late . . . considering the weather.

Stanley spotted him on board the train at Penn Station in New York City. He was very tall, well over six-foot-four or thereabouts because he had to duck, bob, and weave when he boarded the train and while he made his way along the center aisle. He was powerfully built, and with his shaved head, slightly imposing. Stanley guessed him to be in and around forty-five years of age or thereabouts. He took the seat opposite from Annie and Louise Haley. Took his seat, yes, but not before he stuffed his guitar case in the overhead bin. Above all, despite his powerful build, his shaved head, and his height, Stanley noticed the guitar case.

'Acoustic,' Stanley imagined. Something inside the old conductor stirred. He took his hat off, smoothed the two, three, or four remaining hairs upon his head and strutted into the business class car. He made his way, as he usually did, through the quiet car rather quickly.

"Tickets!" He called out once more, for what was likely the millionth time plus ten and one more time that he had called out for tickets.

Stanley took a deep breath; all of this suddenly felt good. He was not sure why, but it did. Perhaps it was the sight of the guitar case.

The last time that he had made his way through the business class car about a half-an-hour earlier, Louise and Annie were enjoying each other's warmth while cuddling up together and sound asleep in their seats. His heart warmed when he spotted little Annie sleeping soundly while clutching the teddy bear tightly in her arms.

Earlier, on the roll, just before Louise and Annie napped, and before the train hit the busy stretch from Newark, New Jersey to New York City, Stanley had shared a little conversation with his two favorite passengers when he had a free moment or two. Within those conversations, Stanley had learned that Mr. Haley was a lieutenant in the Navy and before receiving his latest orders for shipping overseas; his duty station was at a military base just south of Richmond. The family rented a home on the west end of Richmond. Louise added that it was only rental homes for them until her husband finished his career. The military life was too uncertain to buy a home; you just never knew where the next mission would take you to, and Mr. Haley had about four more years left in his naval career. They were both from Hamden, Connecticut, met when they were in high school, reconnected and married shortly after Mr.

Haley graduated from the Naval Academy and received his commission. Louise's parents still lived in Hamden, and that was where Christmas was this year. Learning all about the passenger's lives and sharing in the details might be what Stanley would miss the most of his job. Sharing in the joy, the sadness, and the fun of life. Generally, the passengers openly spoke with Stanley about their lives and their emotions. Stanley Ellsworth was that kind of man. A man that you wanted to speak some words with, share life with, and spend some time with while the train rolled along the many miles. They all were returning home for Christmas. In so many ways.

Where they all used to live and where they still all lived, both in their hearts and in their lives.

The busy stretch was behind them now, and as Stanley had surmised, the train thinned out as they left New York City and some of the stops on the outskirts of the Big Apple behind them. The business class car was especially lean with passengers now.

Now, both mother and daughter were wide-awake and Stanley waved to them and smiled. He could tell that the little girl wanted to speak and unload her latest thoughts on him. First, he had to stop and check the ticket of Mr. Guitar and check in with him, too.

Mr. Guitar smiled and handed Stanley his ticket. Stanley carefully studied his face for a second or two while capturing his every detail. Mr. Guitar was a handsome man. The old conductor glanced at the ticket, then he scanned it and the printer spit out the stub.

"Hartford, Connecticut, huh?" Stanley half-commented and half-asked, although he already knew what the ticket told him that Mr. Guitar's final destination was.

"Yes, I have a gig there. The day after Christmas. On Boxing Day. The Corner Pub in West Hartford. Going to be playing some tunes with a new set of guys. We only rehearsed via the internet. Ya know how it goes these days with electronics. Overdubs and such . . . the Skype and YouTube stuff."

Stanley glanced at the name on the ticket; he memorized the name and then smiled and handed the ticket back to Mr. Guitar. How things have changed since he played so many years ago.

"Well, now, Mr. Craig Miller, that sounds like a great time. I wish you the best of luck. Merry Christmas Eve."

Stanley printed out the stub and stuck it into the stainless-steel rail above the seat. His eyes caught the gleam of the polished guitar case in the overhead bin.

Stanley could not resist but to ask as he gently tapped the guitar case and allowed his fingers to feel the pebble finish of the luxurious case, "What-cha playing here, Mr. Miller?"

"Acoustic lead and rhythm guitar. That is a Martin J-200 up there, ah, ah," Mr. Miller leaned in to read the nametag on Stanley's uniform, "Mr. Stanley Ellsworth. It's an iconic beauty. Holding it in your hands is like holding gold or holding a gentle and fine woman in your hands. Playing it as if you are running your hands over her soft skin, loving her and caressing her every curve. You can generate power and you can generate magnificent tones from it. It is versatile in so many ways. It was the choice of Elvis. Do you know of it, Mr. Ellsworth?"

It was a good thing that Stanley was close to the rail on the edge of the overhead bin because he needed to hold on to the rail for stability. It was not because of a bump or a sway of the railcar, instead, it was because of the tremble of his body. A Martin J-200 was his dream guitar. He longed to play one, but playing one was only in his dreams. The guitar cost a fantastic amount of money and many years ago, all he had money for was his old guitar that he still had in that dusty guitar case in a closet in his home. The guitar that he had not played in forever. Was his old guitar a decent guitar? Yes! Was it a Martin J-200? Well, no way.

Stanley searched for words. Deep inside, Stanley found them.

"I know of it. A very long time ago, in a world far and far away, I played guitar. In fact, now, it seems as if it was ten lifetimes ago. Perhaps, it never existed at all. I dunno, but I played a decent guitar fairly well. I rocked out kinda hard in my day. Yet, I never had the good fortune of playing a Martin J-200. It is the guitar of the king. No doubt. I am not sure that I can even strum a few chords anymore, or pick a few notes or have a style to my playing. It has been so long."

Craig Miller listened carefully to Stanley's words.

He leaned in and smiled while saying, "Playing guitar, if I might," he motioned to Stanley for him to lean in a little and when Stanley did so, then Mr. Miller continued, "Stanley . . . playing guitar is like ice-skating, or riding a bicycle, or playing chess . . . you only briefly wander from the path, but within a few seconds you have it under wraps. You never forget." Stanley only smiled in response to the words from Craig Miller; he gently nodded, waved his hand in his direction, and moved onto the next passenger.

Eventually, Stanley made his way back to Annie and Louise.

Annie jumped on the opportunity to speak with Stanley. She still tightly clutched the teddy bear in her hands while speaking in a Christmas Eve induced enthusiasm, "Mommy says that Daddy can't come home for Christmas this year, but I am wishing as hard as I can that Santa Claus will pick him up in the magic sleigh and bring him to us."

Stanley studied the little girl's face and then scanned Louise's gentle expression, and he sensed the sadness in her eyes too.

"It is as I told you, honey. Santa Claus cannot do everything that children ask of him. He is a very busy man today. It is wonderful to wish and to dream, but certain things, such as the job that your father does for the Navy, are very important and even Santa Claus cannot interfere or help."

Stanley took the stub out of the rail above where Louise and Annie sat and he asked Louise for her ticket while explaining, "I have to re-scan your ticket for the last time. We are down to the last roll." Louise dug around in her purse for the ticket and handed it off to Stanley. While the old conductor scanned the ticket, Stanley explained, "Thank you, Louise. Your mother is correct, dear Annie. I think even if Santa could pick up your father, there might be rules about people flying in the magic sleigh."

Annie pondered the statement and then nodded, as if that made complete sense. She listened carefully to Stanley as he continued to speak.

"Besides, there might not be extra room with all those presents and packages onboard there." Once again, a nod. The little girl was very bright, and Stanley sensed that she reasoned with logic well. As much as a little girl who believed in Santa Claus could use logic! Stanley scanned the ticket, and he waited for the device to print out the stub. He handed the ticket back to Louise. The device coughed out a cardboard stub; he took the scanned stub out of the printer and stuck it in the rail above the seat.

"Do you know something?"

Stanley knelt down in the aisle next to Annie and said, "Your father will be home for Christmas in his heart. A human's heart is very important. It beats to keep us alive, but it also beats in time with love. Christmas is really a holiday to celebrate love. No matter what, whether your father is here right before your eyes or far, far away, he is right next to you, every day, especially so on Christmas Day. You will feel him soon in so many ways."

Craig Miller had been listening in on the conversation from across the aisle. His eyes widened, and a smile broke across his face while stating, "I think there is a song about that, Stanley. Being home for Christmas, missing loved ones, but never being far away from them. Do you know of it? Would you like to take a stab at it on the Martin?"

Stanley weakly smiled and quickly waved his hands in the air as a dismissal of the thought. Yet, the lure of playing the iconic guitar loomed large in his heart.

"I know the song. We used to play it every Christmas gig. Our silly little band. We were The Outsiders." Stanley's eyes sparkled at the memory and his voice warbled and gently trailed off. "It seems like such a silly name for a band now. Anyway, I was the lead guitarist and lead singer. Thinking about it, I now realize how awful we were, but we thought we were good. In some little hole in the wall bars and pubs in and around Connecticut and in neighborhood garages was where we used to live. I lived to play. Oh well, it is part of my past. Great song, but it has been too long since I played and I don't want to be embarrassed. . .."

Annie smiled and asked, "Wow! You can play the guitar and sing, Mr. Stanley! And you know Santa Claus! You are too cool, Mr. Stanley!"

"Thank you. You are pretty neat too. Or, as we used to say, you are a groovy chick. Oh, well, I used to play. A very long time ago and I am not too sure that I can even play a single. . .."

Craig looked at Stanley's hands and noted the size of his fingers.

He pointed at Stanley's hands and said, "You can still play. Those are the hands and fingers of a guitar player."

"Oh, please! Play the song for me!" The little girl's joy erupted in pleas, and her smile at the request shone with her spirit.

Stanley looked around the business class car, and then he reached for his watch and flipped it open. He scanned all the tickets, and the train occupancy was lean and mean. It was the home stretch now. The last roll to New Haven.

He knew they were running about fifteen minutes late, and despite the late arrival, he had some extra time. While he had kept his final ride status a secret to all but the crew, he knew in his heart that this was a special moment. A few other passengers, who were close by and within an earshot of the conversation, stood up, walked over, and encouraged Stanley to try it. Stanley's shoulders sagged, and he grabbed the armrest of the car opposite where Craig Miller sat and squeezed the cushion of the armrest tightly in his hand. That row was a four-seater with opposing seats. A seating arrangement meant for four people to share the ride together and engage in conversation. Only Craig sat there. It was a perfect area to sit and play the guitar.

The old conductor studied the eyes of everyone studying him. Their eyes were wide with Christmas joy, anticipation, and encouragement. Stanley pulled his conductor hat off his head and dropped it in the window seat, and then he slowly sat down in the aisle seat opposite Craig. The emotions were finally running over the top of Stanley Ellsworth.

He ran his hand over his wispy hair and smiled while saying, "My hair used to be down to my shoulders. Can you believe it?" Stanley took a deep breath and said, "I have a secret to share with everyone . . . this is my last ride on the old Ninety-Five. When we reach New Haven, I grab my gear and walk off this train . . . it is over for me. I will retire today. My last ride. My last duty. A lifetime of riding the rails is over for me in about twenty-five minutes."

Louise gasped at the announcement and placed her hand over her mouth. Craig and the other passengers leaned in even more to hear the special news and share at the moment.

"Forty-six years ago, I gave up my dream to play guitar and sing and I joined the railroad. I told my wife it was only for a short time. Until I could play better and sing better and we could save some money, and well, here I am. I wouldn't trade it for anything. Not even to be a rock-and-roll star. Because of this and because of persons such as all of you are." Stanley waved his hands in the air and tears filled his eyes. A few of the passenger's eyes, too. "It has been a glorious life and career. Can you imagine? Here we are . . . forty-six years later."

"Congratulations," several passengers whispered as they studied Stanley for a reaction to their well wishes.

He nodded and fought hard to control his emotions while answering with a low, "Thank you." Stanley lifted his eyes and smiled as he wiped at his eyes with his fingers. "If the offer still stands . . . then I think I will take a crack at that Martin, Mr. Miller. If you don't mind an old hand thumping on your strings. I think I will give the song a try because, yes, we all need to go home for Christmas. To where we all used to live. To dream of the future and recall our past."

Craig Miller jumped eagerly out of his seat, stood in the aisle and, while smiling widely, Craig jubilantly announced, "It is my pleasure, Stanley. In fact, it is all of our pleasures! Come on now, it is Christmas. What a way to end a forty-six-year run. How you began!" Craig lifted the guitar case from the luggage compartment; he set it on the floor of the business class car and carefully lifted the latches of the case. Everyone, even tiny Annie, sensed the reverence associated with this moment and they remained silent and in some awe of the event. They all leaned in while Craig slowly lifted the lid to the case and revealed the precious guitar contained within. A few gasps filtered in and amongst the onlookers, especially so from the Head Conductor of the old number Ninety-Five train, Mr. Stanley Ellsworth. The open case lid revealed the magnificence of the Martin J-200. The lights of the train car reflected on the glorious and flawless finish of the guitar. The strings sat waiting, almost begging for strumming fingers to strike them. They called out for picking, and the neck longed for the fingering of chords.

When Craig Miller lifted it from the case and gently caressed it for a few fleeting seconds before holding it outright from his body toward Stanley, it created an aura around what was going to be the last few minutes working as a conductor for Stanley. Even with the clickety-clack of the train riding the rails and bob and sway of the car, plowing through the snow, the moment seemed frozen in time. The silence was a large part of the beauty.

"Here you go, Stanley. A Martin J-200."

Stanley reached out and firmly, but securely, grasped the precious instrument, and he intently studied it in the lights. He ran his hand up and down the neck of the guitar and then slid it to his lap. At first, it seemed awkward, almost stumbling in his hands, as if he was holding a newborn baby and was afraid of hurting the babe, but after a few minutes of holding the guitar, the past rushed back to Stanley Ellsworth in waves of emotions. Craig reached into the pocket of his jeans, pulled out a wooden guitar pick, and held it in the air.

"Pick?" Craig asked.

"Ah . . . no, thank you . . . I am a flat picker," Stanley said in a low voice just barely audible above the train noise. He looked up at Craig and spoke once again in almost the same level of voice, "Thank you for this. I cannot thank you enough. This guitar is a thing of unparalleled beauty."

Stanley's eyes traveled around and met everyone gathered there, and he smiled at Louise and Annie as they held onto each other.

"Thank you, Stanley," Craig Miller said. "A flat picker, huh? Atkins? Knopfler?" Craig asked.

"Both. You pick 'em. Both are incredible. Neck and neck." With those words, Stanley Ellsworth left the rails behind forever while he gently ran his fingers over the strings of the guitar. A resonance that rode all the way to

Heaven floated into the air. The sound lifted beyond the rails, beyond the metal of the train car. It floated through the air, into the snowy night of Christmas Eve. There, it mixed with the magic in the air and joined in a joyful chorus of celebration of life. A celebration of love, of all that Christmas really means. Craig's words of earlier proved true because it was as if all that Stanley needed to do was to touch the magnificence of that Martin J-200 for everything to return to him once more. There was a slight stumble, a gentle feel of the frets, a slide or two of the fingers and a clearing of the throat. Then it all floated in the air as if the notes were from the strumming of the golden harps of the Herald Angels.

"I'm dreaming tonight of a place that I know. Even more than I usually do. . .."

Patrick, Marcy, and many other passengers from the forward cars heard the news of the amazing musical Christmas Eve concert by Stanley Ellsworth and they all rushed to join in the gathering.

When he finished the song a few minutes later, with the words, "If only in my dreams," that choked with emotions of a shaky but beautiful singing voice immersed with the rawness of a life that was long left behind, it was easy to tell that the railroad gained a hero but, the music world lost one too. Stanley Ellsworth smiled. He ran his fingers over the strings to finish the song on a high note, and he stood up and silently and reverently placed the guitar back into the case and then reached and picked up his conductor's hat. Craig Miller picked up his guitar case and stashed it back in the luggage rack, and he pulled out a business card and gently tucked it into the vest of Stanley's uniform.

"The Corner Pub. West Hartford. Eight o'clock or thereabouts on Boxing Day evening. We need a good lead guitarist and some help on vocals too. We have a set list with some Christmas tunes. Please consider it."

Stanley nodded and patted the shoulder of Craig Miller.

The "audience" clapped and cheered and Annie rushed out of his mother's arms and hugged Stanley Ellsworth around his legs and the old conductor bent over and picked up the precious little girl and held her in his arms.

She kissed Stanley's cheek. He did the same to her cheek, and the little girl proclaimed, "You are the best train conductor ever, Mr. Stanley! That Polar Express conductor only ever yelled, all on board! You play the bestist music ever!"

Stanley set the little girl down, adjusted his uniform, took out his watch, flipped the cover, and he checked the time.

"Next stop in fifteen minutes! New Haven, Connecticut! Union Station!"

Stanley Ellsworth picked up the pace and resumed his duties for the last time.

Stanley completed all of his paperwork and left it for the next Head Conductor to assume the duties for the rest of the trip to Boston. Old number Ninety-Five reached Union Station in New Haven, Connecticut, and Stanley reached the end of the line. He shared a shot of whiskey with Marcy and Patrick; they hugged and exchanged Christmas greetings, warm wishes and promised to stay in touch. We all know how those promises go.

Stanley Ellsworth gathered up his lunch pail, his equipment pack, and silently walked the length of the train one last time. From the lounge car on back to business class. He pushed at the door release, turned and scanned the nearly empty train car. He blinked, tugged at his conductor's hat and then turned and descended the few stairs to the train platform at Union Station in New Haven,

Connecticut. He took a few steps in the snow and turned to watch the train as the engineer blew the whistle a few times and it slowly moved away from the platform and slowly rolled away on the rails and it disappeared into the night.

Christmas Eve was upon the land.

Stanley Ellsworth stood in the cold, in the snow, and in the celebration of a career and of a life. When he turned to walk to the office to punch his last time ticket, it shocked Stanley to come face-to-face with a tall, handsome man wearing a United States Naval uniform. The insignia of the rank of Lieutenant was proudly pinned upon his hat and his uniform's collars. He held a precious Annie Haley in his arms, and a smiling Louise Haley hung her elbow into his. Annie still clutched her precious teddy bear in her arms.

Stanley took a deep breath to keep breathing. The lieutenant handed Annie off to her mother. He clicked his heels in the snow and tapped them together, and saluted Stanley Ellsworth. And since they both wore uniforms, Stanley exchanged and matched the salute.

"Mr. Stanley Ellsworth, Head Conductor, I am Lieutenant Keith Haley. Thank you, sir, for your kindness, your career, your dedication and, mostly, for you. In the Navy, we proclaim fair winds and following seas when we sail off for the last time. I am not sure what you do for the end of a railroad career, but I know, from what my wife and my daughter have told me, you are a special man." Lieutenant Haley winked and added, "You have some mighty pull with Santa Claus because he rode me to my new duty station up the rails a piece in New London. Therefore, for that, sir, and so much more . . . I thank you. Merry Christmas, Mr. Ellsworth."

Stanley smiled, and he coughed out some words, "Former Head Conductor, sir. Now, I am just Stanley Ellsworth. No more conducting. Just an ordinary guy among many guys. Thank you, Lieutenant Haley, for your service and for being a hero. Your lovely wife and glorious daughter made my last ride on old number Ninety-Five memorable in so many ways." Stanley reached out, shook the lieutenant's hand, and said, "Tonight, I have no words, other than wishing you and your marvelous family, a very merry Christmas. Say, I will work a little side musical gig at the Corner Pub in West Hartford on Boxing Day. You know . . . the day after Christmas. It would be my pleasure if you and your wife and Annie could be there. It would mean a lot to me. . .."

Stanley punched his last time ticket; he turned in his required gear to the manager on duty, shook hands with the manager and trudged to the parking lot. He spotted his wife's car idling in the corner of the snowy parking lot. It was still snowing rather heavily. It was a picture-perfect Christmas Eve. The dry snow crunched under his boots, his tracks in the snow were solitary, alone, and the snowy parking lot was nearly empty now. He opened the rear door of the car, tossed his lunch pail and his equipment bag in the back seat of the car, and then opened the passenger's door and slipped into the seat. Stanley took off his conductor's hat and smoothed out the few wispy hairs on his head and then turned and looked at his wife.

"Well, honey, how do you feel?" Mrs. Ellsworth asked and then added, "How was the last ride on old number Ninety-Five?"

"Well, baby, it was memorable, and now, it feels so good that I want to hug you, love you and do everything that we ever dreamed of doing and maybe just a bit more."

Mrs. Ellsworth jumped in her seat upon hearing her husband's words and she sat back while saying, "Well, now, Stanley Ellsworth. Nothing is stopping us. Welcome to the first day of the rest of your life."

The engineer of the old number Ninety-Five train blew the train whistle long and loud. Slowly, the train pulled away from the platform at the Union Station in New Haven, Connecticut. The engineer wanted to make Boston on time. He was only a few minutes late, and the snow was growing heavier and heavier. A few passengers boarded at New Haven, and he would pick up a few more along the way, but for the most part, this roll was happening with a nearly empty train. There was a new crew on board, and after reaching Boston, they would catch some sleep, some dinner, some rest, and then roll on back down the northeast corridor on Christmas Day. The old number Ninety-Five rolls that way. Up and down the coastline, winding its way through twists and turns of the terrain, long soft rolls through gentle curves of the track and hard pounding of the wheels on the steel rails over the long straight runs. Miles upon miles, through the heat and the snow and ice and cold and rain and blazing sun. Old Ninety-Five keeps on rolling. It perseveres. Bringing passengers where they need to go and whence where they needed to return. A metaphor for life, for all of us. We all roll together on the rails of life.

On this Christmas Eve, the train picked up a full head of speed and the snow filtered down, the plow on the front of the locomotive pushed the piles of snow away from the front of the train, and onboard, the passengers settled in for the remainder of the ride.

The train rolled on through the night and the joy and hope of Christmas rolled alongside it. The headlight cut through the falling and now, blinding snow and the wheels of the locomotive and the cabin cars clicked and clacked on the track. On, and on, the train rolled and Christmas peace filled the entire world as Christmas Eve slowly descended upon the land. Peace followed along with the train. All the way to Boston and beyond. That is how it goes with the old number Ninety-Five train.

The train whistle echoed loudly through the snowflakes and the whistle broadcasted joy throughout the land. The sound of the whistle reached high into the air, announcing the mission through the cold and snowy air while adding to the mystique of Christmas as only a lonely train whistle in the night can do. To all those who heard the train whistle, it provided a feeling of peace and calm and added to the joy of Christmas Eve.

Peace, joy, and hope to human hearts.

As only Christmas can do.

Craig Miller's eyes lit up upon seeing Stanley Ellsworth and his lovely wife walk into the Corner Pub in West Hartford, Connecticut, around six in the early evening on Boxing Day. In his one hand, Stanley carried a guitar case; the other arm he kept tucked neatly around the waist of his stunning wife. Stanley nodded and smiled at Craig as Mr. and Mrs. Ellsworth stepped inside the pub and stomped the snow out of their boots. It was no longer snowing, but it was cold out there. It had been an amazing white Christmas in Connecticut, and the holiday festivities just kept on rolling. To be exacting in a description of the weather, it was bitter cold outside; the frost formed on the edges of the windows in delicate web patterns, but it was warm and cozy inside the packed pub. Persons lined up wall-to-wall, pint-glass-to-pint-glass and the holiday lights and decorations merrily glowed in festive beauty. Just outside the windows of the pub, the traffic on New Park Avenue crawled along through the frosty evening. The previous day's snow now lay in plowed piles of glistening beauty along the edges of the world and on the branches of the trees and the structures of the landscapes. On the other side of the road, the elevated tracks of the railroad, stood watching and waiting. Waiting to guide the next train on its way.

Stanley had glanced at the tracks as he passed through the side door of the pub. For the rest of his life there will always be glances at railroad tracks for Stanley Ellsworth.

Mrs. Ellsworth glowed. She had brushed her remarkable white hair out; it tumbled along her shoulders in elegance, and her pride in her man shone like a million galaxies full of the brightest stars. She wore an elegant red dress, very festive in colors and quite form fitting, and it was easy to notice that at even close to seventy-years of age, Mrs. Ellsworth fit out a dress rather nicely. She sported a new necklace around her neck that hung in pride as it announced her amazing cleavage. On the end of the necklace was a small golden train. It was a Christmas gift from her husband.

"I am so glad to see you, Stanley."

Craig hugged and greeted Stanley Ellsworth. His exuberance at the prospect of the old rocker joining his band was overflowing. "This is going to be an amazing gig! Here are the set list and some music sheets," Craig announced as he handed Stanley a paper containing the set list for the performance. "I hope you can read music or do you play by ear?"

Stanley glanced at the set list, and then he thumbed through the music sheets.

"I could read . . . I *can* read music. Yes." He looked up at Craig and then introduced his wife, "Craig Miller, this is my wife, Debbie Ellsworth." The two of them exchanged greetings and Craig followed up the greetings with an invitation.

"Say, Stanley, I was speaking with the guys in the band and I told them all about you." Emotion caught Craig up in some excited rambling, "I will introduce you to them, but I brought along an extra guitar, I see you have yours, but I thought you might want to use my Martin."

Stanley paused; he locked eyes with his wife, who looked up at her husband with a heart full of love and pride. Stanley gently kissed his wife on her lips and Craig admired that even though these two had been together forever, there remained intense love and joy in their hearts for each other. Then again, how could you not love Stanley Ellsworth and all the magic that he brings to the world?

Stanley cleared his throat and explained, "Thank you and that is very nice of you, but because I have the greatest wife in the world, who knew, somehow, that fate would bring us together, I now have my own."

Stanley set his guitar case down on the floor; he bent down and then proudly flipped the latches, pulled back the lid and revealed a glorious and brand new, Martin J-200. The guitar strap even had Stanley's initials embroidered in its folds. The beauty of the guitar glowed throughout the entire pub.

"A magnificent Christmas and retirement gift all rolled up into one." Craig was dumbfounded and his mouth hung open at the beauty of the sight of the new guitar. Stanley stood up, put his arm around Craig and said, "I think the name of the band is kinda cool, the Pub Crawlers, but I was thinking of a new name. How about, The Conductors?"

Craig nodded his head and said, "I love it. Let's go ask the guys what their thoughts are and introduce you and Mrs. Ellsworth. . .."

Outside of the pub the train whistle blew. It sent shivers down Stanley's spine.

Stanley quickly glanced out the frosty window when he heard the rumble of the train on the tracks across New Park Avenue. He could feel the wheels of the passing train shake the floor of the pub . . . right through his boots. His eyes went to the window, and he stared at the headlight of the train plowing through the cold night air. His wife held onto his arm knowing what thoughts were racing through his head.

She smiled and Stanley smiled back.

"Yes, Craig, let's do that," Stanley said as he bent over and latched the guitar case latches and then he stood up and picked up his guitar case and said, "because tonight is the second day of the rest of my life, and man, alive, it sure feels good."

Off in the distance, the train whistle sounded one more time, and slowly, it faded off into the cold night air.

THE END

Epilogue

A light snow was falling at Union Station in New Haven, Connecticut. It was a few days after Christmas and the old number Ninety-Five train was ready to roll south.

Head Conductor Mr. Patrick McGuire leaned out of the train door of the business class car and a few flakes of snow hit his face. A wide smile broke across his face. He looked into the lights hovering above the walkway and squinted in the darkness to admire the fine snowflakes, slowly drifting down and filtering through the lights.

Perfect. It was still the Christmas season until at least a few days after New Year's Day or so, and this was a perfect setting.

His eyes scanned the walkway for passengers. The spry and ambitious conductor walked down the steps and stood on the walkway as the announcements came over the speaker system for boarding of train number Ninety-Five.

A few snowflakes landed on the bill of his train conductor's hat and clung there. Patrick plucked his watch from his belt, flipped it open and checked the time. Five minutes until they rolled south. He could not wait to get rolling. It had been a fantastic holiday. A glorious time!

He and his girlfriend had caught up to his old buddy, Stanley Ellsworth and his musical act at the Corner Pub in West Hartford on the night after Christmas. Boxing Day evening. It was a great show. Stanley had mentioned his love of music, and how he gave up his dream of being a rock-and-roll star for the railroad, but until he heard him sing and play that marvelous guitar on the train, Patrick did not understand how talented Stanley was. The performance at the pub was amazing, especially considering that it was the first time that The Conductors ever played together. Stanley was overjoyed and full of enthusiasm and energy. His wife glowed with love for Stanley and the life that they now had in front of them to live. Stanley and his wife were both back to where they needed to be. Stanley Ellsworth finally returned home for Christmas. For every day.

Where they used to live.

Now it was his turn. Patrick only hoped that he could live up to the legacy of Stanley Ellsworth. Forty-six years is a helluva long time to ride the rails and Patrick could not dream of riding the rails for that long. Life is a long journey.

The train whistle blew loud and long to announce the departure, and the snowflakes fell and drifted in the air while the old number Ninety-Five train slowly moved down the tracks. Patrick hung on the side door handrail of the business class car, enjoying the cold air rushing in his face and making his last passengers and safety checks. No runners.

He resisted screaming out in joy into the cold Christmas air. Maybe on the next stop.

This was it.

The first day of the rest of his life and Patrick McGuire was ready to face all the tasks and all the miles in front of him.

After all, he had a very special teacher and mentor.

ABOUT THE AUTHOR

Eons ago, when the dinosaurs first died off, at the ripe old age of sixteen, Paul John Hausleben, wrote three stories for a creative writing class in high school. Enrolled in a vocational school, and immersed in trade courses and apprenticeship, left little time for writing ventures but PJH wrote three exceptional and entertaining stories. Paul John Hausleben's stories caught the eye of two English teachers in the college-preparatory academic programs and they pulled the author out of his basic courses and plopped him in advanced English and writing courses. One of the English teachers had immense faith in Paul's talents, and she took PJH's stories, helped him brush them up and submitted them to a periodical for publication. To PJH's astonishment, the periodical published all three of the stories and sent him a royalty check for fifty dollars and . . . that was it. PJH did not write anymore because life got in his way. Fast forward to 2009 and while living on the road in Atlanta, Georgia (and struggling to communicate with the locals who did not speak New Jersey) for his full-time job, PJH took a part-time job writing music reviews for a progressive rock website, and that gig caused the writing bug to bite PJH once more. He recalled those old stories and found the old manuscripts hiding in a dusty box. After some doodling around with them, PJH decided to revisit them. Two stories became the nucleus for the anthology now known as, *The Time Bomb in The Cupboard and Other Adventures of Harry and Paul.* The other story became the anchor story for the collection known as, *The Christmas Tree and Other Christmas Stories, Tales for a Christmas Evening.* Now, many years and over thirty-five published works later, along with countless blogs and other work, PJH continues to write. Where and when it stops, only the author really knows.

On the other hand, does he really know?

If you ask Paul John Hausleben, he will tell you that he is not an author, he is just a storyteller. His mission is to continue to write and tell stories to warm your heart, make you laugh, and sometimes make you cry, just a little. Most of all, he deals in memories, and helping you to remember the good times of your own life, and the special people who touched you along the way. Paul was born and raised in Paterson, and then nearby Haledon, New Jersey, and began writing at an early age. He revisited a writing career later in his life, and he now is the author of a number of novels, compilations, short stories and audio and video works. Most of his work, touches upon nostalgic remembrances of simpler times, and tells the stories of heartfelt, humorous, and special human relationships. Other than writing, among many careers both paid and unpaid, he is a former semi-professional hockey goaltender, a music fan and music reviewer, an avid sports fan, photographer and amateur radio operator. He now resides in Somewhere, U.S.A., but his heart always remains along Belmont Avenue in good old Paterson, and Haledon, New Jersey.

Other Work by Mr. Paul John Hausleben

The Time Bomb in The Cupboard and Other Adventures of Harry and Paul

The Night Always Comes, Another story from the Adventures of Harry and Paul

Reunion, A sequel to the Night Always Comes and Another story from the Adventures of Harry and Paul

The Autumn Collection

The Christmas Tree and Other Christmas Stories. Tales for a Christmas Evening

The Miracle Tree, Another story from the Adventures of Harry and Paul

The Summer Collection

Reflections. The Christmas Collection

Christmas Cocktails

Tales of the Quiet Stranger in the Black Hat

Geyer Street Gardens
Beneath the Mask of a Hockey Goaltender
Another story from the Adventures of Harry and Paul
And a few others too!

You may write to the author at ctte27@gmail.com

Follow Paul John Hausleben and God Bless the Keg Publishing LLC on Facebook and enjoy samples of Paul's photography, receive updates on new releases, and enjoy his general meanderings

Published by God Bless the Keg Publishing LLC
Henrico, Virginia, U.S.A.

You may write to the publisher at
Godblessthekegpublishing@gmail.com

"Life's simple pleasures are so often the best ones!"

Paul John Hausleben

www.ingramcontent.com/pod-product-compliance
Lightning Source LLC
LaVergne TN
LVHW050935080826
845145LV00004B/1272

* 9 7 8 0 9 8 8 6 3 3 6 6 7 *